Penguin Crime Fi
Editor : Julian Sy
Hunters Point

George Sims was born in 1923. During the war he
served in the Army's Special Communications
Unit Number One. Since then he has been a dealer
in rare books and has written several novels of
suspense which have been published in Penguins.
He says that 'My books are a mixture of fact and
fiction. I try hard to get the facts right. Readers
must judge the fiction.'

George Sims

Hunters Point

Penguin Books

Penguin Books Ltd,
Harmondsworth, Middlesex, England
Penguin Books Inc.,
7110 Ambassador Road, Baltimore, Maryland 21207, U.S.A.
Penguin Books Australia Ltd,
Ringwood, Victoria, Australia
Penguin Books Canada Ltd,
41 Steelcase Road West, Markham, Ontario, Canada
Penguin Books (N.Z.) Ltd,
182–190 Wairau Road, Auckland, 10, New Zealand

First published by Victor Gollancz 1973
Published in Penguin Books 1976

Copyright © George Sims 1973

Made and printed in Great Britain by
Hunt Barnard Printing Ltd, Aylesbury, Bucks
Set in 9/11pt Plantin (Intertype)

'Death will come on swift wings to him who disturbs the sleep of the Pharaoh'

Inscription on Tutankhamun's tomb

I

Two of the men in the dark blue Dodge Challenger were seated at the front having a quiet conversation; the third man was silent, occupied in dying, leaking blood and life at about the same rate. He was lying awkwardly, half on and half off the back seat which was covered with sacks, wrapped up like a parcel in a tarpaulin stiff with cement dust and boldly stencilled ENTERPRISE CONSTRUCTIONS.

Two of the men in the dark blue Dodge Challenger were seated at the front having a quiet conversation; the third man was silent, occupied in dying, leaking blood and life at about the same rate. He was lying awkwardly, half on and half off the back seat which was covered with sacks, wrapped up like a parcel in a tarpaulin stiff with cement dust and boldly stencilled ENTERPRISE CONSTRUCTIONS.

Sonny Dinsdale, the short fat Negro driving the car, became silent as he concentrated on a decision, while handling the supercharged vehicle like a Bank Manager taking a nervous aunt to church. It was so early in the morning that the traffic was very light, but Dinsdale remained content to follow steadily behind a bus bearing a green poster: SELLINGER FOR MAYOR.

The Dodge Challenger was travelling due north along Van Ness Avenue which in the 1860s was the western boundary of San Francisco but today marks off the down town area.

Dinsdale thought that his companion named Jaeckel understood English quite well for a foreigner but he spoke slowly to him, cutting out most slang words: 'Goddamned cops! You know they killed a coloured boy, Clarence Johnson, right there at Hunters Point the other day.' Dinsdale's bloodshot eyes darkened and his face set in a brooding, menacing expression, then just as suddenly he brightened, grinning at having reached a satisfactory solution to their problem: 'That's it! Ah say we dump this cat at Fort Point. No one 'bout this early, and he don't have to be so much on swimmin' there man. That current there kind of picks you up under the Golden Gate Bridge and then it's good-bye! Straight out in that ole Pacific.'

Jaeckel nodded. The intrusion just after dawn of the two black-and-white police cars into the Hunters Point area had obviously been an unlucky coincidence, nothing to do with their 'contract', possibly related to the death of Clarence Johnson, but it would have been enough to panic anyone in their position who could not remain ice-cool. Both he and Dinsdale were at their best in a crisis but their calmness took different forms, practically light-hearted with Sonny, a feeling of aloof detachment in himself coupled with the sensation that he was in control of the situation and impervious to harm.

Jaeckel half-twisted in his seat to glance at the tarpaulin bundle, then looked at the names of the streets they were passing: Washington, Jackson, Pacific, Broadway. He had been in San Francisco only a few days and none of his time had been spent in rubber-necking, but he had a good sense of orientation and was always checking it in a strange city, doing rough calculations, referring to a mental map and compass; it was an exercise that had proved very useful in the past and was essential in an operation like his present one. Now he could visualize the peninsular city bounded by the Bay on the east and north, and by the Pacific on the west. When they had left the Hunters Point area which was some miles to the south they had headed north away from the wailing sirens and maintained that direction once they had hit Route 101. He guessed that the Oakland Bay Bridge would be somewhere over to his right and that they must be pointed towards the fog-hidden Golden Gate Bridge. It was part of his psychology to be loath to ask questions as it made him appear dependent on someone else, but there were no rules he didn't break from time to time. He lit a cigarette then tested his theory by pointing straight ahead. 'Golden Gate there?'

Dinsdale broke off humming W. C. Handy's 'Beale Street Blues' and shook his balding head. He had been born in Fillmore and still lived there, having spent most of his thirty-nine years in San Francisco, though this included four during which he had been locked up in Alcatraz. 'No, straight on is Fort Mason and Fisherman's Wharf. We make a left on to Lombard, Lincoln, then Long Avenue and Marine Drive will take us to Fort Point. The Fort's tucked away under an arch of the bridge. Mighty quiet there. You might get a few anglers later in the morning but never this early. And it's a military area, the Presidio, so no fuzz.

It's policed by MPs and . . . ' Dinsdale reached out and made a lazy grabbing movement with his left hand – a simple gesture he managed to infuse with considerable menace. 'And if they lucky they won't show.' On the floor of the car, underneath Dinsdale's seat, there was a Colt .357 Python Magnum lying next to a black sap glove in which six ounces of powdered lead was moulded round the knuckles.

Jaeckel turned on the radio half-way through an electioneering announcement which he found amusing. 'Isn't it time someone gives a damn? Politics out of the Department . . . Crack down on hard core crime . . . Have a new city . . . Elect Harold Dobbs Mayor . . . ' Dinsdale did not share his ironic pleasure and snapped the radio off, saying. 'Now this is where we have to take a leetle care man. Ah mus' watch out for that vital turnin'. Miss it and we half-way to Marin County!'

The fog was much thicker on Lincoln Boulevard and it was with some difficulty that Jaeckel spied its name-plate and a blue-and-white seagull sign. The mournful chorus of sirens and fog-horns located round the Bay became ever louder. Jaeckel turned round in his seat and ran his hand over the now inert body in its cement-stiffened shroud. The 'hit' had been unconscious but still alive when they had bundled him up and dashed from the Earl Street house, thinking they were escaping from the cops with only seconds to spare, but no one could take such terrible blows to the head as those delivered by Dinsdale's Colt and survive.

'Kaput now,' Jaeckel said, nodding and retaining a possessive hand on the tarpaulin.

Dinsdale replied in an indifferent voice: 'Not everyone gets well.' He made a right turn into a quiet looking street. 'Well, here we is man! And lookit – we got the place to ourselves jes' lak . . . ' He broke off as he spotted a Yellow Cab in the rear mirror, but it stopped in Long Avenue while they glided along into Marine Drive which took them right to the waterfront, looking grey and mysterious, shrouded by fog.

Dinsdale parked the Dodge as close as he could to the single link heavy iron chain at the water's edge, within thirty feet of the old Fort which had been built in 1861 along the lines of Fort Sumter, but was now dwarfed into insignificance by the massive structure of the Golden Gate Bridge that arched right over it. Unobtrusively he looked round, searching the area, remembering the odd occasion on which he had seen an M P's patrol car parked near by. Satisfied that there was no one in sight, he turned to reach over into the back of the car and began tying pieces of electric flex around the tarpaulin, making it an even more manageable parcel.

Jaeckel got out of the car and walked towards the Fort, experiencing, now that the tension of a tricky situation had ebbed away, a feeling of anti-climax and let-down. Also a nagging suspicion that the job had not been carried out one hundred per cent satisfactorily. He noticed two signs on the Fort, one stating 'No Trespassing 18 U.S. Code 1382' with a penalty of $500, and the other 'No Littering violators subject to fine', and thought of drawing Dinsdale's attention to them but felt that the irony would be wasted on him.

For a moment Jaeckel held his forehead lightly with his finger tips as he concentrated on the events of the past few hours, examining them against a bright screen in his brain as if he was studying old documents under a powerful light; but the reason for his faint apprehension eluded this logical search and he deliberately pushed the matter down into his subconscious to let it stew a while, knowing that this would produce an answer in due course. He began to take in some of the detail of the bridge, surveying the anchorage, noting that the cables were tied down into three massive concrete blocks keyed into one another by a stair-step configuration. He knew that the object of the anchorage was to resist the cables' mighty pull due to their own weight as well as the bridge load. All factual information of this kind was of interest to him. He looked up and tried to estimate the distance down from the traffic deck to the water.

Dinsdale had finished tying the tarpaulin and was satisfied with his handiwork. 'That dude ain't goin' to slip out o' there' he muttered to himself, stepping back out of the car. He shut the door and walked up to the ocean's edge, looking out in the direction of 'The Rock' which he knew had been named 'Isla de los Alcatraces', 'Isle of Pelicans', by Don Juan Ayala, captain of the first ship to sail through the Golden Gate nearly two hundred years before. He had spent four years and two months there in the early 1960s, plenty of time to become an expert on everything to do with the damned place. There was a mixed chorus of baritone foghorns, soprano sirens and grunting bass diaphones. There had been a time when he could make a guess as to where a fog-bank was located just by listening to the characteristics of the signals which all varied, from Point San Pablo to Yerba Buena Island, from Southampton Shoal to Mile Rocks.

When Jaeckel walked back to the car Dinsdale gestured vaguely out to sea. 'That Alcatraz out there, man. Not more than 'bout two and half miles from us and it's less than that to other parts of the Bay. You might think it easy to swim home. But 'member what I told you 'bout that current. In all the time there was a jail on "The Rock" only one man – John Paul Scott – was known to have made it, and they found him half dead. You see, you might be a mighty fine swimmer and you say I'll swim thataway, but the ole current he know best and he say No! try thisaway.'

Jaeckel wasn't listening. His attention was concentrated on the body in the Dodge. He said, 'All right? Now?', opening the rear door and surveying the corpse which had been made into something inoffensive and easily disposable by the stiff winding sheet and electric flex. Jaeckel's brooding suspicion took shape in his next sentence which came to him unprompted. 'He said he'd taken out a kind of insurance. Written something down . . .'

Dinsdale laughed jeeringly. 'That cat was jes' talkin', man. Course he say that. Wouldn't you say that – in his place? No, for a while that cat he want to make trouble, and he give us a hard time, but now he quiet and no trouble at all.'

The two men looked about them. The water at their feet was deep and the freshening wind that was clearing the fog was driving waves against the paved concrete block on which they stood. It was hard to imagine a more suitable or private place for what they had to do. They were practically hidden away beneath the gigantic structure of the bridge while the traffic deck was perhaps three hundred feet above them. The windows in the wall of the Fort which faced them were all bricked up and there was no house in sight. On a fine day their activities would have been observed by passing boats, but the enveloping fog added the final safety factor.

As they heaved the body out, a blood-stained fragment of a spectacle lens fell on the paving. Dinsdale seemed oddly disturbed by this and with a muffled obscenity scooped it up with his free hand and flung it into the ocean. Then they lifted the heavy tarpaulin over the iron chain and with a simultaneous movement launched it into the dark waves. Within a few seconds it had vanished from view.

Dinsdale said: 'Bye Mr Bad News.'

2

An airport is like the world of the future, Edmund Buchanan thought, watching doll-like figures vanishing out of sight on an elevator, listening to conflicting announcements in muffled I-guess-your-weight-machine voices.

While the girl behind the TWA counter dealt with his ticket Mrs Laura Mayhew did not say a word, gripping his free arm and standing so close that he was aware of her body from her knee to shoulder. If she but knew it that silent proximity was her best argument, more eloquent than all the phrases that had poured out during the taxi-ride to London Airport. It reminded him of the nights they had spent in each other's arms, times when he had woken up to watch her sleeping, times in the early hours when they had long whispered conversations and their intimacy gave the sentences they used a special significance.

Too much confectionery, too rich, he thought. It was a terrible lie she had told him, that her husband had 'gone abroad – left me', when in fact he was dying a slow and painful death from leukaemia in Guy's Hospital; the lies that Buchanan had been forced to tell her had nothing to do with their own relationship; her lie affected it vitally. And yet, if he could be honest with himself, hadn't he used the lie to end the affair? Wasn't she too emotional, too clinging, too sensual, too dependent for him – hadn't he begun to find it rather claustrophobic? Too rich, too much, he thought again, pretending to be vitally concerned with what the TWA girl was saying though in fact it made little impact on him.

As she handed over the ticket he did take in something about 'Go on straight up – you've cut it rather fine', but they moved away slowly, ignoring her admonition by walking with a practically slow-motion gait, dictated by Laura's clutching hold.

'Don't blame yourself, if I let you do this to me, don't blame yourself,' Laura said suddenly, gabbling the words as if they had burst out.

He could think of no reply to this volte-face, a strangely subtle reproach, and he walked on grinning foolishly as though they were a loving couple exchanging fond trivialities before his imminent departure.

'Chance of happiness – want some happiness – want it,' she said brokenly.

'We've been all through it, Laura. I'm fond of you, you know that, but I can't keep on seeing you while things . . .'

She used her gripping hand to push him away: '*Now* you're elusive. *Now* you're so particular. At first you just didn't want to know – oh no, you didn't.'

It's becoming like a Punch and Judy show, Buchanan thought, suddenly remembering the beadle, the ghost, the truncheon held in both arms, Mr Punch's repeated phrase: 'That's the way to do it!' It must have been in about 1950, when he was eight, that he'd gone round to the back of the tent on the Weymouth sands, led on by an always strong sense of curiosity, and discovered that Mr Punch's high-pitched buzzing voice was in fact human, achieved by using a 'swozzle', a piece of linen stretched between two flat pieces of silver, bound together with more linen, and placed at the back of Mr Jackman's throat.

Laura pulled on his arm again and turned to face him, giving him the kind of disenchanted look she usually reserved for attractive women. 'Your passport photo does you justice. You're a cool bastard with cold-looking eyes.'

Touché, he thought, but said: 'Don't let's do this, Laura. Just leave it. We'll see . . .'

'See what? Oh, sod you. I give up.' She gave him another violent push in the direction of the TWA girl standing at the barrier with a welcoming smile, and was gone. Noticing the push the air-hostess looked perplexed at this demonstration of female malice. Buchanan grinned at her and walked on towards the passport counter, humming the Sinatra song 'It's oh so nice to go travelling'.

As he walked along the long corridor, which appeared as unreal as a dream landscape, he remembered breaking up with another girl. It had been in Corfu, when he'd been working as a water-ski instructor and girls had come along plentifully. The break-up with one of them had been rather hectic, with a descent to personal abuse on the girl's part: he remembered she had said something about his crowned teeth, meaning to say 'mis-matched teeth' but in her anger saying 'mish-mashed teeth'. So here he was, on Monday 11 October 1971, 'a cool bastard with cold-looking eyes' and 'mish-mashed teeth', one of the very few persons who actually resembled their passport photograph, on his way to the city of San Francisco where warmer people sometimes lost their hearts.

At a bend in the corridor he came to an unmoving queue: it was all part of the airport's 'Hurry up! and Wait!' technique. He felt badly, if a 'cool bastard' could feel, about Laura. She was by instinct a coquette, unfaithful, promiscuous, and an inveterate liar, but she had made him imprudently happy. When he had more time for his own affairs he would see her again.

The queue began to edge forward, to pass in front of a machine operated by the security staff searching for weapons in luggage. Most passengers were burdened with small bags or brief-cases, a few with cumbersome plastic frames containing a frock or long coat which had to be kept uncrushed; Buchanan was empty-handed and would have backed himself on having the lightest bag in the luggage compartment – a small duffle-bag bearing the Union Jack and, rather craftily, on the other side, a Cross of St Andrew, which he'd used during the years when he'd bummed about Europe. The duffle-bag contained three shirts, one pair of light-weight trousers, three pairs of socks and pants, a razor and a tooth-brush, about a third of his worldly possessions.

As he stepped into the Boeing 707, Buchanan mentally repeated Dutch Gaehlen's pre-race prayer: 'Into your hands O Lord and don't make a cock-up of it.' He had been allotted an aisle seat in the no-smoking tourist section which was just behind the first-class area, but he walked straight past it and into the toilet at the back of the plane. It was an unusually warm day for October in England, and the heat and tension of the emotional switch-back ride with Laura had made him feel hot and sticky.

He ran a bowl of cold water and found he had to agree with Laura's verdict on his looks. The other girl had been right too. He'd had four of his teeth crowned after the big shunt; it had been an expensive job and well done; two more had been broken when he'd worked as a bouncer in the Antibes night-club and they were just a little too white. 'Cold eyes', 'mish-mashed teeth', crooked grin. Ah well, he thought, it was the Ugly Duckling story all over again – summer, autumn and winter pass and the ugly duckling discovers that he has turned into an ugly duck.

When he returned to his allocated seat Buchanan found that a beefy-looking man almost as tall as himself was settling into the seat just across the aisle, folding a raincoat with elaborate care. Buchanan hesitated, wondering if he could change seats as there was as yet no one else in the no-smoking area, but the man seemed to know it was his place and moved out of the way with a smile, saying: 'Ah what it is to be young!' His eyes flickered enviously over Buchanan's open-necked check shirt and cheap white windcheater. 'Travelling light, eh! Footloose, and so on. Now look at me!' He lifted a bulky brief-case at arm's length to demonstrate its weight. 'Jam-packed full! Alka-seltzers, travel sickness tablets, pills in case I can't get to sleep, others to inject a little get-up-and-go in the morning. And so forth. Bloody chemist's shop, in fact.'

Buchanan did not relish the idea of an eleven-hour conversation but he had lost his chance of moving without appearing rude. He nodded and sat down, hoping his lack of response might cut off the flow. For a moment it appeared that this had been achieved as the bulkily built man was silent, occupied in stowing away his brief-case, raincoat, hat, magazines and a small packet.

The plane was scheduled to depart at 1 p.m. Buchanan glanced at his watch and saw that it was 1.15, and queried the time with a stewardess pushing a drinks trolley. She got his point and told him that the flight was held up to wait for a group of passengers who were travelling from Lisbon, and that the Captain had ordered a free round of drinks to be served during the waiting period. Buchanan took a beer and stared out of the window, thinking about Mrs Laura Mayhew. Her vulnerable pallor and the hurt look in her eyes had affected him, but anything more

16

than a temporary relationship was out of the question. Somewhere he'd read a psychologist's description of a typical nymphomaniac: 'She's between thirty and thirty-five, possibly with a broken marriage behind her, certainly an unloved, unhappy childhood and a particularly bad relationship with her father, believing she has the *right* to a deeply satisfying orgasm, ever searching for the perfect penis – which does not exist.' Most of this fitted Laura. Buchanan had known lots of women but never anyone else who had got so worked up in the sexual act, behaving each time as if it could be the Sesame to put everything right. Never anyone who had stage-managed the performance with such care – drink, her perfume, the night sky, Beethoven. There had been times when Laura appeared three-quarters 'there' on those ingredients so that his part in taking her, in her phrase, 'over the top', appeared no more important than Mr Alfred Brendel playing Beethoven's Piano Sonatas.

Buchanan shook his head as he stared heedlessly out of the window; it was an unconscious movement, prompted by a feeling of amusement and something else – probably admiration. What a woman she was! He had not liked leaving her like that: when she had cried in the taxi he had felt that all the guilt was his. It was a messy business making love to a woman in between her visits to her dying husband, but he should have found some other way of breaking off, lied his way out so that she was not hurt so much. It was odd that she had not asked him how he had discovered her husband was in the cancer ward at Guy's Hospital.

'Well, that's that. And about time, you may well say. I frankly envy you. Each time I fly I intend to walk on the plane empty-handed and I always end up with everything.' The tough-looking man, who appeared as much in need of a 'chemist's shop' as Muhammad Ali, had finally put away all his gear and turned round to stare reflectively at Buchanan. 'Ever done this particular trip before?'

Buchanan shook his head, then added 'First time' in a way which was not planned to encourage further chat. The big man was persistent, continuing to stare at him and saying vaguely: 'Something or other . . . Yes, something or other.'

Hearing that phrase depressed a switch in Buchanan's brain so that adrenalin was pumped in, like the moment before the flag-start in a race when he was seated dressed only in fire-proof underwear and overalls, but he gave no sign that all his attention was now firmly concentrated on the man who suddenly pointed and said: 'Ah yes. Got it!' in a tone of self-congratulation, as though he'd caught some rare specimen. 'You're Ed Buchanan. The racing driver. Right?'

Buchanan said: 'Guilty. But you must read the small print. I was never in the headlines ... '

'Too modest! Much too modest! I can remember your name with those of Beltoise, McLaren, Jochen Rindt ... '

'Now you've overdone it,' Buchanan replied. 'I wasn't bad, but I definitely wasn't that good.'

'Wasn't? You've given it up?'

'Vice versa. It gave me up. I had a bad shunt and didn't get back afterwards.' This rather vague, modest-sounding explanation always went down well and satisfied anyone who inquired. Sometimes Buchanan wondered if he would ever tell anyone that the real reason he had stopped racing had nothing to do with his own crash, but was the simple result of his parents being killed when their small car met a lorry head-on. Some psychological hang-up prevented him saying this.

'Oh yes. The crash. Monza wasn't it?'

'No, the Ring. Nurburgring in Germany. A tough one. Thirteen miles of twists and turns. Your car leaves the ground – all four wheels – perhaps seven times in a lap.'

The burly man leant across to shake hands. 'Name's Jack Collier. Are you staying in Los Angeles or going on to San Francisco?'

'San Francisco. Partly a holiday, partly with the idea of looking round for a job. I've been selling cars and my brother – he lives in San José – has the notion I might get a good job there in San Francisco. He thinks I might like the place too. So I decided to have a look see.'

In the past few months Buchanan had found that he had a reasonable talent for telling lies. He liked this one about the non-existent brother: he had brother Andrew living in a quiet part of

San José – Buchanan could visualize him there, living in a new house high up where he got a beautiful view of sunsets; becoming a little heavy, drinking beer from the can, thinking of taking out papers for U.S. nationality.

'Yes, it's a beautiful place. Beautiful,' Collier said in an unenthusiastic voice. 'Say, if you're in car sales now you could probably suggest a good one for my boss. He wants to buy something rather special. Price not too important. Small, sporty, preferably exotic. Male virility symbol I suppose.'

'How about the Dino Ferrari 246? Smallest Ferrari there is – a two-seater sports. Driving position excellent and better all round visibility than you'd expect. Fast – a genuine 140. Definitely exclusive – only about one hundred of them in Britain. Costs over five thousand but not an expensive car by Ferrari standards as their next one, the Daytona, costs over nine thousand . . .'

'Enough, enough! You've blinded me with science. But I'll take a note of that name.' Collier took out a tiny notebook and jotted down a few words. While doing so he said: 'This trip goes on a bit you know . . . Advertised to take eleven hours to L.A. but it's often longer against a head-wind, then there's a forty-five minutes at least wait till we take off again for San Francisco, and we shall follow the sun so we'll have it with us all the way, and also we lose eight hours. When you eventually get there it's about eight in the evening local time, but by your old internal clock it's four ack emma, lowest ebb time . . . ' Collier seemed to have depressed himself with these dismal prophesies. He put his notebook away, finished off his glass of gin, then sat fiddling with his safety belt. After a while he inquired casually: 'Where are you staying? I shall be at the St Francis. Give me a buzz one evening and we'll have a drink in the Piccadilly bar there.'

Buchanan thanked him and said he was booked into the Hotel Jerome for four nights. The Hotel Jerome in Post Street.

Collier looked a little puzzled by this. 'Post Street? Really? Funny – that's where the St Francis is, down near Union Square. But I don't know the Jerome – must be up at the other end, on the edge of the Chinese quarter. In that case you'll probably find it's run by Chinese. None the worse for that though. Very efficient, business-like people . . . ' The sentence petered out as though Collier had lost interest in the conversation; he swivelled round in his seat and waved an empty glass.

Buchanan had been taking in details of Collier's appearance and mannerisms: he was just over six feet in height and looked as if he weighed about thirteen or fourteen stone; his face was unlined and his dark brown hair was still thick, but Buchanan estimated his age as fifty. Collier crinkled up his face a lot in smiling but the blue-grey eyes remained watchful; his hands were square, his fingers stubby with the nails cut so short that no white showed at the edges. The hand not holding the glass was balled up into a fist.

The pilot began a pre-take-off announcement, apologizing for the delay, and Buchanan fastened his safety-belt and lay back with his eyes closed, thinking about his tiny flat in Wapping. He had not added a thing, apart from a few clothes, to the bare essentials provided by his landlady. After his parents had died he had sold most of their belongings and sent the remainder to his only surviving relative, an aunt who now lived in Edinburgh. If someone was to search his rooms in the bleak Tench Street house it would be an unrewarding job, like coming up against a blank wall. In his mind he performed a scrupulous examination of the seedy premises, including the oddly shaped bathroom-cum-larder. When he approached the wardrobe it was with a tiny jolt he remembered that he had left one personal item in his only suit – Laura's last, passionate letter, written with a faulty fountain-pen which had blotted the page till it looked like a mysterious diagram.

3

Tony Bellimo made his one big catch in an otherwise undistinguished angling career on 11 October 1971. That Monday, which was to figure largely in Bellimo's conversations during the following months, always being referred to as 'my longest day ever', began in a routine way but ended with sleeping pills and then a nightmare so vivid and frightening that it woke him from his drugged sleep.

Bellimo, a widower, had lived alone in a small apartment on Columbus Avenue since 1969 when his daughter had married and moved to Carmel. As a boy, before the war, he had worked with his father at the agricultural community at Asti; from 1942 to 1946 he had served in the U.S.A.A.F. without leaving the States 'or ever hearing a gun fired in anger'; after his discharge from the service he had been employed as a waiter at various restaurants in San Francisco. His present job at Alioto's was the best but also the most demanding he had found; in his fiftieth year he realized he needed to take it easy on his day off.

The nine-day 'British Week' had ended on 9 October, and it had been a particularly busy period at Alioto's Restaurant as Fisherman's Wharf had been buzzing with 'Cheerio, pip pip and smashing' voices, and many of the Britishers had wanted to try the famous Alioto specialities – cioppino, clam chowder, Rex sole, calamari and coo coo clams. When he awoke on the morning of the 11th Bellimo felt bushed and dropped his tentative plan to visit the Farmer's Market on Alemy Boulevard where he occasionally shopped for vegetables, and stayed in bed for an extra hour, rising at nine a.m. to make some coffee and read the papers.

After this frugal breakfast Bellimo drove from Columbus Avenue to Geary in order to take a few photographs of the impressive Saint Mary's Cathedral – it was a long promised chore, a favour for a friend of a friend of his cousin who had helped to build the cathedral's organ at Padua. He took some time out there simply sitting in the sun admiring the audacious architecture of the cathedral and staring up at the baldochino of free-hanging aluminium rods. He little dreamt that a brief account of his morning was to be included in the following day's issue of the *San Francisco Chronicle* and a fuller one in *L'Eco d'Italia*.

From the cathedral Bellimo drove to Fort Point to do some fishing. The only kind of local angling he considered exciting was surf-casting from Bakers Beach from July to August when the stripers were running, but he found a few hours down by the Fort relaxing even if his catch was usually negligible. He had with him a loaf of sour-dough bread, some Italian dry salami, tomatoes, a peach and two cans of beer for a picnic lunch, and carried his binoculars in case the fish weren't biting.

Bellimo arrived at Fort Point shortly after eleven a.m. By the end of the day he had been questioned so many times, both by the police and reporters, that he became a little confused about some details of the morning's events, but he did remember checking the time because he felt hungry as soon as he had parked the car and had glanced at his watch then.

There was only one other man fishing near the Fort, a retired mail man named Vorpal, with whom he'd exchanged a few remarks. Vorpal gave a dismal thumbs down verdict on the fishing prospects and Bellimo put his rod and line together in a leisurely fashion, singing a snatch from the song 'Mimi'. He had recently seen the old Maurice Chevalier film on TV and had been pleasantly surprised by its gaiety and charm. He had particularly enjoyed seeing that old Britisher C. Aubrey Smith waking up in the morning and surprisingly bursting into Chevalier's song:

> Mimi!
> You naughty little good-for-nothing Mimi
> Am I the guy?

Bellimo felt lethargic and rather apathetic about fishing that morning, largely because Vorpal had not caught anything. He walked along to a spot he usually favoured, practically under the bridge, and cast out his line a short way, then propped his rod against the heavy iron boundary chain, keeping the butt in place with a stone. The cruise-boat *Harbour King* was just passing as it turned under the bridge. Bellimo waved at some sightseers on board. The ebb tide looked as if it was at its peak, probably running close to five knots. He took out his binoculars and walked past the Fort to scan the boats hugging the Marin Peninsula near Point Diablo. There were lots of catboats with vari-coloured sails, two yawls, a sloop and a fine old schooner, with its distinctively tall after-mast, running before the wind and probably heading for Sausalito. The bare hills and sunlit sea made a perfect background for the flurry of sails.

When Bellimo returned to his rod he thought at first glance that his hook must have caught on a rock. He reeled in some line and then tentatively lifted the rod to test this notion. Vorpal called out to ask if he had caught a fish. Bellimo shook his head, reeled in a little more line, then struck gently first one way then the other in the hope of disengaging the hook. When he held the line tight he was puzzled by his conviction that whatever the line was hooked into lay just below the surface of the sea. As he stood pondering on this, more or less resigned to losing the tackle, a movement of the waves disclosed that his line had caught on to something white that looked more like cloth than a rock. Bellimo called out to Vorpal who came along to hold the rod. With his binoculars Bellimo could see that his taut line ran down to a curious looking sack. He handed his glasses silently over to Vorpal and they exchanged suspicious, slightly anxious looks.

Leaving Vorpal to hold the rod Tony Bellimo ran back to his old Chevrolet and was beginning to back out from the parking bay when he spotted an MP's patrol car in the mirror. He ran over to them, waving his hands. One of the MPs returned with him while the other went through a gate which led into the Fort, returning in a few minutes with a grappling iron and chain.

The long sodden sack, tied with black flex, was very heavy and the four men practically had to wrestle with it in order to get it up on to the concrete block. By the time they had done so they all knew that it contained a body though no one said anything. Bellimo was torn between a feeling of aversion and one of fascination as the tall MP Sergeant with a morose expression knelt beside the tarpaulin and untied one of the strands of flex. There was a strong smell of seaweed, with which the tarpaulin had been festooned, and something more pungent, like rotting fish.

When the Sergeant pulled back one flap of the sacking it first resisted his action then gave way with a sucking sound. Bellimo, against his will and with a deep shock of nausea, took in the frightening aspect of a man's head from which the face had been ripped off like a Halloween mask by the adhesive mixture of cement, sea-water and cloth. It was this 'terrible peeled face' vision that was to be the subject of Bellimo's nightmare that night. He turned away groggily from the apparition, walked a few paces on numb legs, then knelt down on the wet paving stones and vomited.

San Francisco has the highest suicide rate in the United States, and enough murders to keep a large and efficient Homicide Department busy twenty-four hours every day in the year. There is a code of procedure that is invariably followed when a body is discovered. The MPs told Bellimo and Vorpal to sit in their cars while they reported the matter to the local police station. Within five minutes an Emergency Ambulance had reached the scene, the body had been examined and death officially pronounced. Two black-and-white San Francisco police cars arrived within the next few minutes, one with a Captain and a Sergeant from the local station, the other containing Homicide Squad Inspector Frere and Sergeant Pickering.

It was Al Frere, a deceptively mild-looking giant, who questioned Tony Bellimo. From his first glance in Bellimo's direction, a glance that Frere had come to rely on through hard-worn experience, he was convinced that he was dealing with an innocent bystander, just someone unlucky enough to be on the spot, but certain facts had to be recorded right away. Frere got down all the details as quickly as possible, then suggested that Bellimo should sit in his car and take it easy.

By this time the area by the Fort was more crowded than at a peak holiday period. Members of the Mobile Crime Unit and the Photography Unit were busy at work, there was a large crowd

24

of MPs, and the uniformed members of San Francisco Police Department were arranging for the area to be temporarily cordoned off. Reporters from the *Chronicle, Examiner, L'Eco d'Italia, Le Californian,* and the TV programme 'Eye-Witness News' had arrived. Sergeant Pickering was conferring with an assistant from the Coroner's Office about the removal of the body.

Left alone, Tony Bellimo lay back in his driving seat, half-closing his eyes, then sprang out of the Chevrolet to stand up and stare at the cloudless azure sky in an effort to rid himself of a horrific inner vision.

4

Edmund Buchanan's exceptional strength and quick reflexes had served him well in his brief motor-racing career but they had induced a temporary delusion of superiority: subsequent events had dealt with this conceit; indeed the effects of the cure had been stronger than the illness so that while he had roamed round Europe he had often felt sorely inadequate. After leaving school at sixteen he had worked in a garage then joined the Metropolitan Police as a cadet, leaving it after three years' service, which had been followed by a further period as a motor mechanic, finally graduating from the pits to driving Formula Three cars. All of his working life had been largely bound up with physical activity and he was aware of the gaps in his education and the absence of a cultural background.

Buchanan's application to join the Special Branch in the summer of 1970 had been viewed sympathetically partly because of his family's long connection with the service, and his father's 'sterling record', but he also believed that he had made out quite a good case for having originally joined the police as a youngster without giving the matter much thought, and now feeling strongly about the work of the Special Branch.

Attending lectures on Political Science had underlined the sketchiness of his general knowledge but had shown him that on the plus side he had good powers of concentration and observation; gradually he was becoming more self-confident again, and this new confidence was better founded than that which had been built solely on muscle and quick reactions.

On the morning of Tuesday 12 October 1971 Buchanan woke in San Francisco at six a.m. local time, showered, dressed and went out for a walk before breakfast. In Sutter Street he found a garage where he bought a street map, strolled down to Union

Square and then back up Post Street, thinking about his programme for the day. Allergic to sight-seeing, as he was to so many things which other people found pleasurable, he had nevertheless to establish his identity as a man who had come to see the sights of San Francisco as well as with the idea of seeking a job there.

When he returned to the immaculate Coffee Shop in the Hotel Jerome to order coffee and poached eggs on toast, Buchanan thought how puzzled Mrs Laura Mayhew would be if she was there to study his reactions to being a tourist. His response to most cultural activities from ballet, for which he preferred the East End Londoner's description 'Pouff's Football', to the theatre had always rankled with her; she had probably finally written him off as a philistine when he had asked her to turn down the record of Alfred Brendel playing Beethoven's Piano Sonata in A flat major. Now his attitude to the tourist attractions of San Francisco was like that of a man who dislikes bathing but feels he must have a quick dip while staying by the sea.

From the foyer counter in the hotel Buchanan had picked up a booklet *Key*, adorned with a photograph of Princess Alexandra, issued for the benefit of visitors to the city during the 'nine-day British Week festivities' which had finished on the previous Saturday. He flipped through this quickly and decided that a taxi tour taking in Nob Hill, Telegraph Hill and all the North waterfront from Fisherman's Wharf to the Golden Gate Bridge would provide him with some kind of tourist background. Then he would go for a walk round Chinatown which he knew he would enjoy. Living for some months in the East End of London and often eating at Chinese restaurants there he had come to admire the Chinese as a race – this was a strong feeling with him so that he had not needed a few encouraging words on the subject from Jack Collier. He had never known anyone in Limehouse well enough to say that he liked them, but he had a feeling of respect for the Chinese people in general and would be interested to see what they had made of their enclave in San Francisco.

Returning to his room on the fifteenth floor, Buchanan locked and bolted the door then sat down at a table-cum-desk, took out some sheets of the Hotel Jerome writing-paper, and set himself an examination question for he found that making notes was his best way of marshalling his knowledge of a subject. The imagined question was 'Write notes on the life of Abe Resznik':

Abraham Isaac Resznik. Born at Nikolaev, 1892. Known to have been a member, while still in his teens, of a Marxist group, led by Alexandra Sokolovskya, her brother Ilya, Dr Ziv and Lev Davidovich Bronstein (later Trotsky). Arrested in February 1910 and sent to Siberia. Escaped or released in 1912 and believed then to have left Russia for Finland (period from 1912 to 1918 during which time he married Ziva — is not documented). Returned to Russia in 1919. There is a photograph of Resznik in Georgia that year, taken at the height of the civil war, in which he is seen posed with Trotsky, Trotsky's wife Natalya and Arkadi P. Rosengoltz, a member of the Revolutionary Military Council who later became *chargé d'affaires* at the Soviet Embassy in London and was executed by Stalin in 1938. Secret employment (intelligence/counter espionage?) for Resznik from 1920 to 1929 when he is said to have finally left Russia. One son Arkadi Resznik born 1920. A curious photograph exists showing Abraham Resznik with Trotsky and Trotsky's wife at Prinkipo after Trotsky had been banished from Russia. On this snapshot Resznik's image is half deleted in red ink and the word *provocateur* is written by it in Natalya Trotsky's hand. Resznik is believed to have lived in the Baltic States during the early 1930s and then in Hamburg till he left Germany as a refugee in 1937. Resznik reached London in October 1938 and settled in Stepney, working at the St Katharine Docks from 1938 to 1952. His wife Ziva was killed when their house in Orton Street was bombed in 1940. His son Arkadi and daughter-in-law Chana-Mindel are presumed to have been killed by the SS during the forced march of 650 survivors from the concentration camp at Sachsenhausen in April 1945. Resznik's grandson David, then aged 11 months, was rescued by the Swedish Red Cross when the marchers halted in the Below Forest and was in the small party sent in a guarded convoy, reaching the Allied lines at Schwerin on 3rd May. David Resznik lived in various DP camps till September 1946 when the British Red Cross arranged for him to be sent to England to live with his grandfather.

Buchanan could have written an equally lengthy and detailed piece on David Resznik's life, but that information he had researched recently and he did not feel any need to refresh his memory about David who as a potentially dangerous revolutionary seemed to be a pale shadow of his grandfather.

If Buchanan had been asked as a second question on his

imaginary paper to write down his reasons for seeing Abe Resznik as a potential threat to Britain or any democratic capitalist society he would have found it much more difficult than the recital of known facts concerning Resznik's past, but he was convinced of it. On the surface it appeared absurd. Resznik, a myopic frail old man, quietly living on a small pension in a council flat in Wapping, was not a member of any political party. He was said to have joined the British Communist party in December 1938 and to have been expelled from it six months later. Abe Resznik rarely left the borough of Stepney and appeared to spend his mornings in taking gentle exercise by walking and shopping, his afternoons reading, emerging after tea to spend two hours or so in one of the half-dozen pubs near by. Occasionally he would enter into arguments on political subjects but gave the impression that he was operating at half-throttle, holding back his real feelings. Buchanan knew that Abraham Resznik had sat in on some secret meetings of the Angry Brigade, and then no doubt he had been able to express his opinions freely. But there had been the odd occasion in public when Resznik had let slip some indication of his long frustrated feelings about capitalist society.

It was true that Abe Resznik was nearly eighty and often in poor health, physically feeble, still limping slightly from an injury he had sustained when his house was blitzed, and having no influence with any properly organized political party, and yet Buchanan thought that he could be labelled potentially dangerous, whereas most of the boys shouting for urban guerrilla warfare were full of hot air.

Buchanan had gradually become fascinated by the character of the old man, which was like an iceberg in that so much of it was hidden – there were so many enigmatic gaps in Resznik's past that would never be filled in – he had led an extraordinary life, yet posed as a simple dock-worker pensioner. His grandson David was a different kind of person, equally intelligent but highly vocal and articulate. There had been a stream of political articles written by him since he was a schoolboy.

While the only visible indications of Abe Resznik's feelings were an occasional smouldering look or a much more rare comment, these had to be linked with his past in which he had performed the dangerous acts of a revolutionary, spy and *agent provocateur*. Edmund Buchanan admitted to a grudging feeling of admiration for Abraham Resznik but viewed him as a kind of human explosive which could still be detonated. No doubt Resznik's revolutionary ardour had been subjected to countless periods of frustration and disenchantment, nevertheless he was still a force to be reckoned with and Buchanan was not surprised that the young hotheads called the Angry Brigade had sought Resznik's counsel.

Buchanan burnt his notes on Abe Resznik, sent the ashes fluttering from a window, then went down to the hotel lobby in the old slow-moving lift, secretly amused by the thought that he had been given the brief of watching Resznik and his youthful contacts as a piece of beginner's work, a routine task which a tyro could handle, and now there were signs that it might turn out to be more important than his superiors had guessed.

Buchanan walked up Post Street to Van Ness Avenue and made a note on his *Key* booklet of the addresses of two car firms specializing in sports models, then hailed a Veterans cab driven by a colourful looking hippy, and asked for a quick tour of the highspots. He did not intend to alight at any of them, but to be driven along by his lackey, a veritable symbol of the effete capitalist society.

5

El Paraje de Yerba Buena – the place of the good herb – was the name originally given to San Francisco, from the mint that grew profusely in the surrounding sand-dunes. Today it would be impossible to find a phrase to describe this complex city.

The discovery of San Francisco Bay was an ironic accident. In 1769 an overland expedition set out from Mexico to extend the Spanish colonization of Alta California. The expedition kept close to the coast except when forced by mountains or other natural obstacles to make a detour, and it was in this way that the Bay was found by Don Gaspar de Portola. In 1775 the first ship, the Spanish Navy's *San Carlos*, entered the Bay. Inspector-General Galvez had told Father Junipero Serra, 'If Saint Francis desires a mission, let him show us his harbour and he shall have one': in 1776 *San Francisco de Asis*, the mission in honour of Saint Francis, was founded, and near to the mission, on a strategic promontory, a presidio or fort was built.

Mexico did little about this most northerly of its territories and over the years it became continually more neglected, and in 1846 an American Naval Captain John Montgomery raised the Stars and Stripes over the settlement. Its rapid growth as a city was bound up with the discovery of gold in the El Dorado County, and the fantastic mountain of silver, known as the Comstock Lode, in Nevada, by which such men as James Fair, John Mackay and William O'Brien became fabulously wealthy and started a frenzy of financial activity. The symbol of great wealth in the 1870s was Nob Hill where tycoons like Charles Crocker, Mark Hopkins and Collis Huntington strove to outdo each other in the magnificence of their mansions. When a hotel was built in 1925 on the site of the castle that had been Mark

Hopkins's attempt to create his own Xanadu, a half-million gallon reservoir was discovered in the courtyard.

In the earthquake and following fire of April 1906, four square miles of the city were destroyed. The threat of future earthquakes has not stopped the traditionally optimistic Californians from building a city of just under fifty square miles on the most improbable of sites, a series of hills.

Today San Francisco is a city of paradox in that its great financial area around California and Montgomery Streets, dominated by the towering Bank of America, is only a few blocks from the 'Skid Row' section below Market Street: it encompasses palatial housing areas on Pacific Heights and Sea Cliffs as well as degrading slums like Butchertown and Hunters Point.

Hunters Point is the name of a headland, between India Basin and South Basin, that was chosen as the site for the San Francisco Naval Shipyard. The shipyard is a U.S. Naval Reservation strictly prohibited to the public, but the name also covers the housing area near by. In the early 1940s, during the wartime boom in the shipbuilding industry, hundreds of 'temporary' houses were erected there. As the industry declined in the following decade many of the workers moved out, and the vacated houses were taken over by Negro families. In a country whose god is change Hunters Point took on the blighted air of a district left to stagnate as the prosperous citizens went elsewhere.

Today Hunters Point is an illustration of the urban sickness that has attacked the United States: roads leading to it pass through an industrial wasteland of disintegrating workshops and half-demolished factories, acres of old cars left behind when auto-wrecking firms went bankrupt, and empty lots strewn with concrete blocks, rusting wire, matchwood and piles of garbage.

Two violent events, a gang war of youths in 1961 and a riot five years later, have marked its history, but at the present time violence erupts there in the form of crime; policemen have been assassinated while driving through the area and they approach the place with caution. There is massive unemployment amongst the largely Negro population and many of the younger generation are drifting in a world of enforced idleness, poverty and drugs.

A block away from the bustling corner of Third Street and Palou Avenue, where the War on Want offices stand, there is a curious relic of another era – the South San Francisco Opera House, built in the nineteenth century, which remains empty for months on end though occasionally used for community performances or as a rehearsal hall for some struggling rock band. The side of the Opera House facing the community centre of the Burnett School is used as a kind of notice board, with scrawled, rambling messages in chalk and staccato statements in spray paint: 'Dope', 'Kill or be killed', 'Anthony was here', 'Dope can be found here', 'Kill whitey'.

On most days of the year a few citizens from Hunters Point will find their way to the Hall of Justice which is on Bryant Avenue. On the corner of Seventh Street and Bryant Avenue they pass a large piece of abstract sculpture and then are confronted by a handful of firms offering a Bail Bonds service.

The Police Department Administration Bureau, the Criminal Courts and Traffic Courts are located at 850 Bryant Avenue. There is a notice at the front door: 'All people entering these premises are subject to search. Wait behind ramp . . . ', and the search is a careful one carried out by experts, but once past this barrier the atmosphere is relaxed, there is a Candy Shop on the ground floor, and the police on duty in the building give an impression of being distinctly human.

The Homicide Department is on the fourth floor, in Room 450. There are in fact three rooms: two small ones for the Lieutenant in charge of the department and two female secretaries; a large one for the detectives.

On 12 October 1971, the day after the faceless body was found at Fort Point, Sergeant Harry Pickering was seated at his desk near the Emergency Information Notice Board, filling in an Incident Report on the case. He had been forced to leave some of the sections blank, and he knew that if the fingerprints of the faceless man were not on record they were going to have a difficult job in establishing identity.

The angler's chance discovery of the body at Fort Point had a dramatic quality and for that reason it had been given some space

3

in the newspapers, but the public would have forgotten it within a week. Now was the time when police activity would pay off best but it was hard to get started without a single clue about the victim. Pickering left the form incomplete and stood in front of the main notice board, staring at a large scale map of the Presidio area.

'Have a nice day.' Pickering turned round on hearing the ironic greeting from Al Frere. 'The coroner confirmed the kerbstone diagnosis. The man was dead.'

'Thanks a lot.'

'Massive traumatic injury to the back of the head. Weapon a pistol butt, a large Colt. Been in the ocean three perhaps four days. Something else. And this might be a help.'

Frere produced a transparent plastic bag. 'The kid had a secret pocket sewn in those Levis, and there was a small wallet in that pocket, and I think that wallet was waterproof.'

'Say not so.'

Frere tipped a green plastic wallet on to a blotter. It was secured by a wrap-around flap and Frere opened this with a nail-file, exclaiming: 'There! What I said. See those bills!'

In one section of the wallet there were ten dollar bills so little dampened that they could be easily separated. There was also a compartment of the wallet that was fronted with a piece of clear plastic devised as a ticket pass holder. This contained a faded photograph of a man and a woman standing in front of a wooden house. Frere extracted this by pulling on one corner and found a blue piece of paper behind it, a September page torn from a current diary.

Frere turned over the photograph to find there was nothing written on the back, and then stared at the piece of paper. He said slowly: 'Yes sir! I think this one is going to drive us out of our skulls.'

On the page of the diary the names Oakland, San Francisco and Los Angeles were written in black ink below each other, with the figure 10 repeated at the side. Then the number 30 followed by a large, elaborately doodled dollar sign, a question mark and an arrow pointing to the initials F.W. and another arrow pointing to the word Quicksilver.

Underneath there was a pencilled note:

quick'sil'ver (kwĭk'sĭl'vẽr), n. [*quick* living + silver; from its fluidity;
cf G. *quecksilber*, L. *argentum vivum*. See QUICK, adj.] 1. The metal
Mercury. 2. A mercurial, esp. an elusive person or thing.

6

'All right, pal?'

'Fine, thanks.'

Buchanan found it difficult to keep his face straight at this second solicitous inquiry. Murray the hippy cab-driver had turned out to be a surprisingly mild character. Behind the disguise of a grubby Mickey Mouse shirt, straggling beard and pigtail of hair tied up with a black ribbon there was a frustrated tourist guide. They had taken only two intersections at enough speed to make the cab momentarily lose contact with the road, but both times Murray was glancing back. The brief tour Buchanan had outlined had been considerably developed by Murray, but he had given value for money with a detailed explanation of how the cable-cars worked from a continuously moving steel rope, travelling at about eight miles an hour, the connection between the cars and the cable being a pincer-like device called a grip, noting that only 17 miles of track and 39 cars remained. Buchanan also now knew that an old chocolate factory in Ghirardelli Square had been turned into a complex of shops, galleries, plazas, steps and restaurants. The extended tour had taken in the Golden Gate Park, a glimpse of the City Hall and a more protracted viewing of the Haight-Ashbury area which had once been internationally known as a Mecca for hippies but was now, according to Murray, 'over-run with blacks, hard drugs and bad scenes'.

Buchanan asked for the only address he had memorized in San Francisco, the house in Laguna Street where David Resznik had boarded until 4 October: he half-closed his eyes and concentrated on the problem posed by Resznik's disappearance. Buchanan had long thought that the rationale of motor-racing or any dangerous sport was that it made you raise the ante of effort and concentration to the utmost so that for a while your actions became deadly serious and your mind was cleared of trivial thoughts. His work for the Special Branch had a similar effect, but he felt that if he was to find David Resznik he would not only need his powers of concentration but also a good measure of luck.

On 4 October, David Resznik had walked into the British Consulate General's office on Montgomery Street in San Francisco, stating that his life was in danger and he needed help, vaguely substantiating this by saying he had got involved in some illegal activities that were out of his control. While the official who interviewed him had left to find a security man, Resznik disappeared from the building. Inquiries by Consular officials at the Laguna Street address had resulted only in their being told that Resznik had 'gone off but without indicating where'.

Murray did not seem to realize that the guided tour was over and half turned in his seat, speaking out of the side of his mouth: 'Say, I meant to say in the Haight, we didn't get to see any of the steepest streets yet. The toughest to climb are Filbert between Leavenworth and Hyde, Arguello between Irving and Parnassus, and 22nd between Church and Vicksburg. Want to try one?'

Buchanan said: 'Thanks but no thanks. I'm supposed to be in Laguna Street just about now.'

Murray gave up, nodded and said: 'Okay . . . okay. Only two minutes from here.'

Haight-Ashbury had been a rather seedy area but they were now travelling through a quiet street in a pleasant residential part of the city with houses in varied styles, a number of them having eccentric touches like a witch's hat turret, a fanciful cupola and an extra large circular window with a cartouche. The sky was clear, the sun was warm and Buchanan felt as relaxed as if he was just a tourist – his mood was right for making a seemingly casual inquiry at the Walters' house.

The cab went past an oblong plot of greenery which Murray identified as 'Lafayette Park', turned into Laguna Street, and they pulled up by a row of houses that Buchanan guessed must have belonged to the pre-earthquake epoch, roughly dating them as Victorian by the sash bay windows, the wooden filigree work, and elaborate iron railings guarding the steep steps to the front doors.

Buchanan gave Murray a generous tip, making free with government money, then looked round at the city of San Francisco stacked up on itself to the South. In the brilliant sunlight it had a luminously tiered, faintly Oriental appearance. The only noises to be heard in Laguna Street were a mimic starling's rambling cries and children's laughter. He turned to survey the Walters' house before retreating behind his dark glasses. It was large and attractive, double-fronted and on three floors, part of the lower floor being below street level. Lots of the windows were open, with clean curtains moving in the breeze. The front door was open too, and as he went up the steps he smelt the delicious odour of a stew cooking which made him suddenly hungry. It was an old-fashioned bell and he could not hear it ring, so that he stood for a few moments wondering whether he should also bang on the door.

Two small boys, both in pyjamas and dressing-gowns, appeared silently at the back of the hall. They had pale faces and their hair was darkened with water and brushed straight back. There was something odd about their expressions but at first he could not place what it was. As they came closer to the door he saw that they both had artificial fang-like teeth protruding from their mouths.

'Does Mr Resznik, David Resznik, live here?' Buchanan asked. The boys said nothing and Buchanan changed his tactics. 'Is your mother, or your father in?' The boys remained silent like miniature models of Dracula, both regarding him gravely with mouths clamped shut.

'You boys! You know you are *not* supposed to go downstairs. Not, repeat not. Who is that at the door? Boys, are you deaf?'

A tall, attractive woman in her late thirties came down the stairs. She had dark brown curly hair, and lively brown eyes with an amused expression; she wore a slate-blue pinafore frock over a white roll-neck pullover. She smiled when she saw Buchanan confronted by the miniature Draculas. 'I'm sorry about this. You see it's a dreadful programme they watch on TV.' She waved them upstairs. 'Up you go. *Now*. You know you're still supposed to be in quarantine.'

When the boys had vanished she explained. 'They had mumps but the time limit has just about expired . . .'

Buchanan cut short her apologies by saying succinctly: 'Had it. Mumps I mean. Look, I'm sorry to bother you but I wanted to see Mr Resznik, if that's possible. He does live here?'

The tall woman nodded and her expression became serious, looking very much like that of the two little boys. 'He does indeed. Are you a friend of Dave's?'

'No. But I know his grandfather. My name's Buchanan. Ed Buchanan. I live just round the corner from Abe Resznik in London, off the Wapping High Street. He's been worried about not hearing from David so I said I would look him up. I'm here on a short holiday . . .'

'Come in, please come in. I'm Sally Walters. The charming smile appeared again, reinforcing Buchanan's opinion that David Resznik had been fortunate in his choice of lodgings. She held out her hand. 'I'm glad to meet you. I've heard so much about Abe that I feel I know him. I've been meaning to write to him . . . It's a difficult situation . . .'

Sally Walters indicated one of the doors leading off from the hall. 'Do you mind if we talk in the kitchen? There's something cooking I must just look at. And I'll make some coffee – if you'd like that.'

'Very much. I'm a coffee addict. What did you mean by "a difficult situation"?'

He followed her into a large kitchen with a long unvarnished pine table and eight chairs round it. There was a matching pine dresser bearing lots of plates and rows of red jars with the names of spices written on them in white paint. Something was grumbling and jostling in a saucepan on the stove. The piquant smell of stewing onions and meat was an added inducement to move from the Hotel Jerome to Laguna Street.

Sally Walters removed the saucepan containing eggs from the stove and put on a kettle. 'It's disturbing. About Dave. That's why I haven't written to Dave's grandfather really. I don't know what to say you see. Dave walked out of here a week ago yesterday

– in the morning – and we haven't seen him since. I expected him back for supper that night and he just didn't come. No message. Nothing. And it's quite out of character too. I mean, he's a bit footloose and liable to take off, but he's always told me . . .'

Buchanan didn't relish telling her lies, but he had always known there would be things about his job not quite to his taste. 'Yes, that does seem very odd. Abe Resznik was concerned because he hadn't heard from David for some time.'

Sally Walters sighed. 'Oh dear. That would figure because for the two weeks before he went off Dave was in a whirl of activity, flying to L.A. – and back and forth across the Oakland Bridge like he couldn't stop. So I suppose he just didn't get down to writing Abe then. And those letters to and fro between them used to be as regular as tick tock. It all becomes worse the more I think about it. You know, in a situation like this you turn every which way but it doesn't get you anywhere.'

'None of his friends have any idea where he may have gone?'

'No. He's close to a girl who's staying here temporarily. Cherry Kinsella. She's an Anglo-Irish girl, and lives in London, but she's been over here on an extended vacation. She's just plain mystified about Dave – like I am. But the main reason I'm so worried is that the very day he went off I had two men from the British Consulate call here in the evening, saying they wanted to see him. And they've phoned every day since checking on whether he's back.'

'Couldn't that have been something fairly routine?'

'No, I don't think so. They asked to see his passport and I showed it to them. But Dave has this Exchange Visitor Visa – a J1 they call it – a special one for foreign faculty and research scholars. That's quite okay. Anyway they wouldn't send two men to inquire about a visa – one asking questions and one saying nothing, just watching me. Like cops.' As she talked she was going through an automatic routine of making instant coffee in a blue-and-white striped jug, putting out bowls of cream and sugar. Buchanan was enjoying sitting in the spacious kitchen where everything looked so workman-like and clean. He had often found that the atmosphere of expensive restaurants inhibited his appetite, but seeing Sally Walters busy by her stove had the opposite effect.

When she handed him a cup she said confidingly: 'I think Fred Wheeler may be the joker in the pack. He might have got Dave involved in something wild. They're great buddies and he lives in Berkeley – that's across the bay – where Dave has been spending so much time lately. The clincher to my theory is that Fred seems to have vanished too.'

Buchanan was searching for a formula, trying out various approaches mentally, to justify a persistent interest in David Resznik's fate that would not appear suspicious. He was given a moment's reprieve by a child's shout or scream that rang out from above. Sally Walters moved quickly to the door and listened intently. The shout had been accompanied by a thudding noise, but it was followed by peals of childish laughter. She raised her eyebrows in mock despair, saying: 'Kids!' As she came back to the table she smiled. 'I said that but really you know, what a sane world kids live in! I was thinking just that when you rang the bell. Going through David's things, I thought how sensibly children live and what complicated messes we make of our lives later on.'

Buchanan said: 'I hope you'll have good news of David soon. I don't like the idea of going back to London and having to say to Abe that his grandson has vanished just like that. I feel I ought to find out more – if I can.'

'Okay – if you feel like that – fine. I felt I might be going on too much about it. I mean, you being on vacation and only knowing Abe casually. But if you feel at all concerned . . . Look, come upstairs. I was just tidying things in David's room. Have a look round with me. We might find something, a kind of clue.'

They went up a wide staircase. There were five doors on the landing and from one of them came the sound of a man's voice in what sounded like a monotonously-keyed speech. Sally pointed to the door, saying, 'That's Cherry's room. She's listening to KPFA – a listener sponsored programme, very serious, with lots of "concerned" talk and no adverts. Makes a change from KJAZ,' she added, pointing to a silent door, 'which is what we usually get there. Solid jazz, and hours of it.'

She unlocked the third door to disclose a sunny room with bare white walls. There was a divan bed covered with a Mexican or Indian rug, an unvarnished pine wardrobe and a small desk covered with papers and books. White-painted shelves along one wall were full of books too, and they overflowed on to the floor in tottering piles. Propped up against one shelf there was a very large photograph of a young man: profile and full-face shots of a striking face surmounted by a luxuriant head of curls. Buchanan instantly recognized the full lips and the bold stare partly obscured by a cordless pince-nez. It was a much enlarged reproduction of a 'mug shot' of Lev Davidovich Bronstein, the romantic-looking youthful Trotsky, which had been discovered in the files on dangerous revolutionaries kept by the Secret Police in Imperial Russia.

Sally walked over to the crowded desk. 'I've been through everything here. No guilt about it because Dave knows I've never been in the least bit nosey about his affairs. It's different now.' She picked up a small photograph and stared at it intently. 'Where the hell are you, Dave?' she asked rhetorically.

The shelves were crammed with books on politics and looked like a section of the Agitprop bookshop in the Bethnal Green Road. Buchanan had seen much of the material before, but the piles of newspapers and magazines were largely local student productions. He moved behind Sally to look over her shoulder at the snapshot of two young men and a girl. One of the men he knew was David Resznik, though he had grown a wispy beard since his London days. The girl was tall and attractive with unusually large eyes. The other young man looked like a shorter version of Resznik with similarly long hair, straggling beard and super-relaxed posture. 'That's Dave with Cherry and Fred Wheeler – the buddy I said had also vanished . . . ' She stared thoughtfully at Buchanan for a moment as she came to a decision. 'Can you stay for lunch? Cherry will probably be having it with me and I'd like you to meet her. Only a pot-roast but kind friends have told me that I make it fairly tasty.'

It was an invitation easy to accept. Buchanan grinned, saying, 'Fine. I'd like that. I thought I smelt something delicious when we were in the kitchen.'

Sally was moving papers about on the desk in a half-hearted fashion as if she was already despaired of finding anything useful. 'Cherry's quite a character. A free spirit. Lives on her boat *Shamrock* in the middle of London, or so she tells us. The boys are intrigued about that. They think she may be fooling them. I suppose you can moor a boat in Maida Avenue?'

'Yes, on a canal. Rather a nice way to live. The sensation of being afloat and one minute's walk from the shops.' Buchanan replied abstractedly as he was looking at the massed papers on Resznik's desk with considerable interest. There was so much material that it would be impossible to make a proper search without arousing Sally's suspicion. He noticed a pile of newspaper-cuttings as they lay beneath a magnifying-glass which focused attention on the word FRENCH. They were mostly extracts from the financial columns of various American newspapers and the *Wall Street Financial Magazine*, with a few pink snippets from the British *Financial Times*. The top one was concerned with a rumour that the financial backing of a French industrialist group, Garve-Schweber, was behind the emergence of a new Texas oil firm; the next one was a study of the complex structure of the House of Krupps – the only linking theme seemed to be the general one of high finance.

There was a noise on the landing and then the sound of someone running down the stairs. This was followed by the sound of a scuffle and youthful shouting. Sally hurried out of the room and a moment later Buchanan heard her calling out: 'Oh Cherry! You're not going out are you? Can't you have lunch here? I want you to meet . . . ' There was a quiet reply to this which Buchanan missed as he walked out on to the landing.

A tall girl with long red hair was standing by the front door holding one of the small boys at bay by pushing at the smooth forehead beneath the smarmed down Dracularian hair. She wore lilac-coloured trousers with a matching long sleeveless jacket over a high-necked ivory silk blouse. Her face was pale and there was a curiously sedated look about her which Buchanan found sexy.

Sally was standing half-way down the stairs and she made a hurried introduction. 'Cherry, this is Ed Buchanan. He knows Dave's grandfather. Lives near him in Wapping. Can't you possibly stay for a few minutes if you can't manage lunch?'

Cherry Kinsella gave Buchanan a long, slightly glazed stare as if she was trying to get him into focus while shaking her head. 'No – alas! I have to rush. Just had a phone call, and it's important. So must go. Sorry . . . ' She gave the small boy an affectionate push and used her forefinger to implant a kiss on his immaculate parting. After this she looked once more at Buchanan – there was a long seeming moment of mute interrogation before she said: 'I must dash. Someone's waiting – but I hope to see you another time, Mr Buchanan.' Before he could reply she had gone.

7

'Get out your worry beads man.' Inspector Al Frere said this to himself as he stared at a graph showing the times of onset and duration of the principal post-mortem changes which was pinned on to the Emergency Information Board in the main Homicide Department room at the Hall of Justice. 'This is sure a going nowhere case.' He had gathered various bits of information on the Fort Point murder case but they could not be made into a pattern. 'And if it don't gel then it ain't gelatine,' he mused aloud. Most homicides were committed on impulse and to a detached observer at first seemed haphazard and pointless, but later on it was usually possible to make some crazy kind of sense out of them. Earlier in the summer he had been involved in a case where two black narcotics had been shot dead in a desperate attempt to raise funds for heroin. They had both been unarmed, and it came to light that they had been butchered simply because of their too insistent demands for cash. Such a homicide was at once absurd and yet made a pattern, whereas the facts they had ascertained about the victim at Fort Point just did not fit in with what was obviously a professional killing.

Frere stopped brooding on the post-mortem graph and transferred his attention to an Information Bulletin poster relating to a planned attack on the Ingleside Police Station that had taken place in August when Sergeant John Young had been assassinated. There was a composite drawing of a female, another of a 9-millimetre rifle and, rather tantalizingly from his point of view, front, rear and side aspects of an auto, Chevelle 1971 model, dark green colour. If only that Mrs Gunter had been a shade more observant. Frere moved across the room to another notice board which was covered with jokes and fake notices, touched the yellow plastic chicken which was suspended from a ribbon, then looked over the glass partition of the small office in the corner and saw that Lieutenant Green was momentarily alone. You could often take him a close-tangled skein of wool and he would prise out a loose end.

After picking up some documents from his own desk Frere knocked on the Lieutenant's half-glass door and held up a hand to illustrate his question. 'Can you spare five minutes Lieutenant? This Fort Point case?'

'No problem,' Green replied, beckoning him in. 'Take a seat. Fact is I wanted to bounce something off you.' He pointed down to his blotter on which there lay cuttings from the *Chronicle* and *L'Eco d'Italia*. 'This guy – this Tony Bellimo – the guy who hooked the body. Anything?'

'Bellimo? Oh, he's Mr Clean himself. Seems to work harder than most at being a nice guy. Couldn't find a whisper against him anywhere.'

'Any luck with your inquiries in the Presidio area?'

Frere noticed that the Lieutenant's desk was clear apart from the cuttings and the blotter, in the corner of which were tucked some pages from a jotting pad. He could see from brief notes in Green's stylishly clear hand that the Lieutenant had evidently been giving the case some thought: one below the other were the names Bellimo, Vorpal, Enterprise and Quicksilver, while the initials F.W. were written in slightly larger letters and vigorously underlined.

Taking the cigarette offered by Green, Frere said: 'I thought we had struck oil there. That close. In Long Avenue we talked to this dame – a Mrs Gunter – who remembered seeing a car going in the direction of the Fort very early in the morning of the 7th. It stayed with her because apparently it's very unusual to see any traffic going past her place that early. It seems she'd just flown back from a wedding at Bakersfield and a Yellow Cab brought her home at about 6.45 a.m. A dark coloured, newish model, she said it was, but no idea of the make or any guess about the registration. Our luck is that she's a dame who's not in the least interested in cars. So I checked back with the cabby but nothing more. In fact, with him . . . ' Frere shook his head from side to side, implying doubt. 'The cabby said only maybe. He thinks he *may* have seen it.'

'This Mrs Gunter – she's not the type, you know, who reads the papers and thinks wow! if it happened that close I must have seen something?'

'No – I'm sure she saw it, but it doesn't help much. I spent half-an-hour going through a mass of photos, but even now she wouldn't know the rear-view of a Chevelle from a Volkswagen. But what she did say fits in just right with the timing the coroner gave us. He had a lulu of a job with this case, but finally settled for a twenty-four hour period that covers that night of the 6th and part of the 7th. He said that the victim died in that tarpaulin. With any luck it could have been the perfect crime. A shot in a hundred that the body snagged those rocks. The weapon . . . the method of disposal . . . and everything . . . makes it a pro job . . . ' He came to a faltering halt as he realized he had drifted into the obvious.

Green murmured 'Yeah, yeah' then looked up to ask: 'Nothing on the prints?'

'Negative. We checked them out with L.A. and Washington. But we think the guy may have been British . . . '

Green moved his head slowly to one side, opening his eyes wide, in a way that indicated Frere's narrative had reached its peak of interest for him. 'How so?'

'Well, his denim shirt and the cord Levis could have been bought locally, but his briefs, socks and sneakers were all trademarked "St Michael". Now that's a brand name used exclusively by the British chain stores Marks & Spencer. And he's got fillings which our forensic people swear are European.'

'Give me his physical description, Al.'

'Height six one, weight 130, hair brown, thin build. Fair complexion. Myopic – very much so in his left eye. They found a fragment from his specs that had been driven into the cornea. Callous on his index finger that makes it look as if he did a lot of writing. Whatever he did he didn't make muscle. Puny kind of undeveloped frame . . . '

Green pondered the significance of the facts he had been given in encapsulated form, then said: 'So we had this recent British invasion, and now it looks like one of them might have got nailed to climax his trip. But what a target for a bit! He's a desperate son of a bitch, no muscles and blind without his specs. He interests me, Al. What did he do – or was it something he had? Do you see the way my wheels are beginning to turn, Al? Go see the British Consulate people over on Montgomery – check on whether they've had any reports on any of their tourists going missing. Then check with Pan-Am, TWA and BOAC about any Britishers not taking up return flights to the U.K. Yes, I know that's liable to turn into quite a chore. So tell Harry I want you to take plenty of time over this one. Oh, by the way, two more items. What about the photo the kid had in his wallet? And anything on the tarpaulin?'

'We won't get anywhere with that tarpaulin, Lieutenant. Belonged to a big construction firm, Enterprise Constructions Cemaceco, that operates all over the state. And they lose scores of those wraps every month. Now, the wooden house in the photo that the kid carried was European but *not* British. Probably Russian or one of the Baltic states.'

'You're closer than you think, Al. Just a little luck now and you'll tag him. And I've a feeling about this one – it's going to lead us somewheres else.'

8

It had not been difficult to steal the diary from David Resznik's room. Buchanan had noticed it, half-hidden by some unused foolscap sheets of paper, as he looked through the collection of financial column cuttings on Resznik's desk. As soon as Sally Walters had gone out of the room to speak to Cherry Kinsella, Buchanan had pocketed the diary. When Cherry left the house in Laguna Street Buchanan had returned to Resznik's room with Sally and recommenced searching with her, experiencing a pang of guilt rather than anxiety for she was too nice a person to suspect him of taking anything.

After some minutes of haphazardly moving round papers on the cluttered desk Sally had produced an engraved card, 'OCEAN-EXOTICA INC. Leonard Troy. Corner of Polk and Geary, San Francisco', on the back of which there was a scrawled message in green ink, 'Bien, Dave. Hopefully we'll see you here Friday about eight for some of the pain-reliever doctors recommend most. Jerry.' She had given it to Buchanan saying: 'That's from a good friend of Dave's, Jerry Harland. A very nice boy. He works at Leonard Troy's shell-shop, lives there too. I've called Jerry a couple of times since Dave took off, but nothing. At least, he said he had no news though he sounded rather cagey. Perhaps you might look in there if you're passing. Who knows? He might tell you something that he would keep from me.'

An hour after leaving Sally Walters's house Buchanan was seated on the wooden verandah of a bar overlooking Fisherman's Wharf, nursing a beer and going carefully through the diary. The first flip through had been disappointing as it had shown that the diary had not been used in a conventional way, but merely recorded a few place names, figures and initials.

The only coherent body of writing occupied the first few

pages which should have chronicled the daily events of January 1971. This was headed 'Groups in Berkeley' and went on: 'YSA is the Trotskyist youth group. In all matters of policy it is guided by the major Trotskyist party, the Socialist Workers Party. Marxist critics often accuse the YSA of moving in on other groups with no strong ideological basis and attempting to control them, and are critical of its "busy bee" activity . . . PLP is a national Maoist group, smaller than YSA, less orientated towards youth, addresses itself principally to the industrial working-class – hence its short hair and no drugs, a working-class kind of puritanism . . . YPSL (members are called Yipsels) has only a small campus group. The YPSL is a shadow of its former self. An interesting group in the late 1950s and early 60s when it was quite influential. Today it is closer to the Democratic party than any of the other left groups. Basically dull and conservative . . . The IS (pronounced Aye-Ess) is a national Marxist group, composed mostly of students and other young people. Its intellectual origin was in the 1940 split in the American Trotskyist movement. In that year perhaps 40 per cent of the SWP split off to form the "Workers Party". The intellectual giant of the Workers Party was Max Schactman who felt, at the time of Russia's invasion of capitalist Finland, the necessity for a new appraisal of the Russian system. Trotsky himself took a part in this discussion, taking the line that the Soviet Union, though a "degenerated workers' state", was still, as a workers' state, to be defended in any wars with capitalist nations . . . '

All the notes were in a similarly brief form, giving information without much opinion and no padding. This, together with the fact that they had been written in a diary, led Buchanan to believe that they might have been composed on one of Resznik's numerous trips to other cities in California. It might have been material for an article, but it seemed more like an analysis of the radical scene in Berkeley prepared to show to someone who knew nothing of the subject.

Buchanan went carefully through the other pages up till September, checking again that they were all blank. It was at the beginning of September that Resznik had got canght up in a whirl of activity, travelling constantly to Los Angeles and

Oakland, always adding a mysterious numerical notation by place names or by initials on each entry in the diary.

The numbers joined many other imponderables in the David Resznik affair, but Buchanan thought a reasonable guess would be that they represented payments and that Resznik had been acting as paymaster in some conspiracy which needed considerable financing. That was as far as supposition would take him, and even that was a ramshackle bit of building which would probably collapse immediately new facts came to light. He still found it difficult to account for Resznik's double change of heart which had taken him into the British Consulate to ask for help, then out again before it could be offered, leaving only an impenetrable puzzle behind him.

Buchanan finished his beer and put the diary away in a trouser pocket. The sun was so hot that he had taken off his windcheater jacket, and had been walking in shirt-sleeves like most of the men in the crowds thronging the waterfront. The sky was cloudless, and the sea-reflected light was so glaring that his dark glasses were essential. From the wharf there came the inviting sounds of rigging blown against masts and the sea slapping against the hulls of fishing-boats. Sea-gulls screamed overhead as other pastel-coloured boats chugged their way back to the wharf. As a faint continual chorus there was the distant buzz of the crowds milling past stalls where they were offered 'Walkaway Cocktails' of shrimps with sauce in paper cups, and crab vendors standing in front of steaming cauldrons calling out: 'You want it cracked?' For half-an-hour Buchanan had been part of the throng being tempted by crab-meat chunks sprinkled with 'Thousand Island' dressing, walking round The Flying Scotsman which was on display on the Embarcadero, and staring at the superb metal-hulled square-rigger Balclutha moored at Pier 43. Mingling with so many family groups, overhearing children's excited comments at what seemed to them an extraordinary railway-engine, had quite dissipated Buchanan's usual aversion to sightseeing, and for a while his sense of loneliness had gone too. Basically it was his feeling for families who wanted to lead ordinary peaceful lives, 'the cosy lives of the bourgeoisie' which he had heard arrogantly denigrated by a number of revolutionaries, that had brought him into the fight against those who would use bombs and kidnapping to achieve political ends.

'We go the way our fathers went.' The opening line of the half-remembered poem came into Buchanan's mind as clearly as a church's leaden bells he had heard earlier that day with their admonitory salutation: time is passing. The verse knapsack that Buchanan mentally carried was light, consisting of a few lines from Burns and Omar Khayyam, and he did not feel any need to add to them, but this one poem was returning to him more and more often with a strong message.

Ten years before he would have thought there was no similarity between himself and his father: when he was twenty he had tended to look down on his parents' rather humdrum, suburban lives, the pleasures of which had been bounded by gardening, walks with the dog, and television. His father had been a reliable but unambitious man who had only reached the rank of sergeant in the Metropolitan Police after twenty years' service; he was amiable and imperturbable in a crisis, but at twenty Buchanan had found even his father's virtues irritating. Now he could see a lot of his father's character in himself, principally a dogged persistence, a kind of blinkered determination to finish any job that had been started. Now there was also more of a physical resemblance, and he recognized some of his mannerisms as being inherited too. Occasionally he would use one of his father's stock jokes or sayings.

Leaning on the wooden railing at the edge of the verandah, confident he would not be overheard, Buchanan repeated all that he could remember of the poem:

> We go the way our fathers went
> Despite their tears, entreaties, blame
> Beneath the self-same burdens bent
> We go the way our fathers went

Several factors and events over a quite long period had contributed to Buchanan's decision to inquire whether he could obtain employment with the Special Branch, but he could remember the exact moment when the various reasons had fused into a definite desire on his part. Returning to England after a long period of travelling aimlessly round Europe, taking any job that had the momentary appeal of something new or exciting, he had started to work for a car firm. One day, after demonstrating an Aston Martin to a potential customer in Chichester, he had been caught in a cloud-burst at Midhurst and pulled up to have tea at a café crowded with families travelling to and from the seaside. Sharing a table with a family divided in their allegiances between 'Farmhouse Tea' and 'Devonshire Tea', he had read in a newspaper about a bomb left by a revolutionary faction which had killed a woman and maimed a child. At that moment his long smouldering antagonism to revolutionaries who made a cult of violence had taken hold of him, as firmly as though his father had shaken him by the shoulder.

Buchanan had lived through the same period as David Resznik; like him he had a working-class upbringing, going to a state school in a rundown part of London; like him he was disturbed by glaring social inequalities, and he knew where his sympathies lay between industrialists and those who had to count the money in a purse before buying groceries, but he was resolutely opposed to anyone willing to use bombs, kidnapping and the haphazard terror of so-called 'guerrilla warfare' to change the existing social order.

In his search for the man who had vanished Buchanan thought that every fact he could add to his store of knowledge about Resznik might eventually help, so he began to review the scraps of information he had picked up in his visit to the house in Laguna Street. David Resznik did not smoke or drink, had a meagre appetite, 'being hardly aware of what was set before him', obviously something of a sore point with Sally Walters. Resznik had no interest in clothes, but had a strange penchant for wearing tennis shoes. He was not keen on any sport but made a point of taking the Walters boys to watch baseball; it was plain he was a favourite with them, and they probably regarded him as some kind of substitute for their father who had been killed in a plane crash. Resznik had hardly any personal possessions apart from his books; he had a solitary relic of his parents, a faded photograph which he always carried with him 'as a kind of talisman' – this was the way Sally Walters had put it, but she had probably adopted the phrase from Resznik. The photograph of Arkadi and Chana-Mindel Resznik, butchered by the SS because they were Jewish, was certainly a salutary reminder of a loathsome régime; but Buchanan was not clear exactly why Resznik regarded it as a talisman, unless he thought there was a continual threat from the forces of fascism and saw his own revolutionary activities as being directed against it. Buchanan thought it was illogical to cling to one totalitarian regime in order to oppose another, but as he discovered more about Resznik he was convinced of the strength of that perverted idealism.

9

The façade of Ocean-Exotica Inc. was eye-catching with viridine green lettering shaded laterally on a light green background, but at first sight it appeared that the premises might have been cleared for removal or redecoration. When Buchanan glanced at the shop as he stepped from a cab at the corner of Polk and Geary Avenues he thought the window was bare. Approaching the door he saw that there was an austere window display; someone had made a half-hearted attempt to represent a strand of beach with starfish, an anaemic-looking crab and some pale-ribbed shells. At the back of this artificial beach there was a small cabinet with a tray pulled out to disclose more exotic shells. One large shell was placed on top of a sheet of eau-de-nil paper with the firm's engraved letter-heading and cable address, 'Starbuck, San Francisco', and a few words in green ink, 'Triton's Trumpet. Charonia Tritonis. (Linné, 1758)'.

Opening the door produced quite an elaborate response from electric chimes but no one appeared to answer their summons. A small desk and chair were pushed right into the corner of the shop as if they wished to retreat from the hurly-burly of trade, and two fragile chairs faced the desk. The carpet was sea-green, very thick and luxurious. A massive globe of the world and a gaudy green parrot in a stainless steel cage completed the furnishings. There was no sign of any stock, and it appeared that the business must be conducted on the lines of an expensive jeweller where desirable items are produced for suitable clients. The magnificently coloured parrot ducked its red crest but continued to eye Buchanan suspiciously and move about uneasily.

Buchanan thought it would be inappropriate to call out 'Shop!' and looked round to see if there was a bell that could be used to attract attention. He noticed that the door in the middle of the wood-panelled wall facing him was just ajar. He pulled this half open and looked along a passage to see the back view of a heavily built man standing engrossed in a phone call, saying, 'Oh my God no!' and making an effeminate gesture as though to ward off bad news. Buchanan moved back a little but he could still hear the man saying: 'No sir! I like to stand back from the heat. Way back!' More words were lost when the parrot suddenly did an eerie imitation of a human laugh and squawked: 'Freak. Freak.'

Buchanan strained to pick up more of the conversation in the passage. 'Jerry was talking to this very important person. We'll have to do it his way – understand? Yes, we'll be in touch. My God though . . . . Okay. Yes. So long then.' There was a sound of the telephone being replaced, and Buchanan moved silently back to the middle of the shop. After a minute's silence he heard the voice in the passage again. The words 'Say it isn't so' were half spoken, half sung.

Buchanan cleared his throat very loudly, like a bad actor, just before the parrot squawked: 'Freak out.' A moment later the door in the panelling was opened by the heavily built man, who wore tight grey cord trousers and a fancy cowboy-style shirt with white piping and mother-of-pearl buttons. He had a deep tan and the rigid profile that boxers display when they've had their face repaired too often. He had made a quick recovery from the bad news; he flashed a showbiz grin, saying: 'Hi there! Can I help you?' The voice was husky and suspiciously deep and masculine, as if he worked at the effect.

'Mr Troy?'

Leonard Troy acknowledged his identity with another grin but managed to convey some slight reluctance, like a celebrity who thought he might be asked for his autograph. His light grey eyes were taking in every detail of Buchanan's appearance. 'Yes, I'm Leonard Troy. Is it business?' He waved his hand vaguely in the direction of the shop window.

'My name's Buchanan, Ed Buchanan. I was hoping I might have a word with Mr Harland. I've just been to see Mrs Walters.'

'Sally Walters over on Laguna?'

'That's right. She suggested I might look in. I'm over here on a short holiday. I know David Resznik's grandfather in

London – I live in Wapping just a street away from him – and I thought I'd look up David.'

Troy's face clouded and he nervously stroked his impeccable grey hair. 'I get the picture. So Sally told you that Dave has split – er, gone off into the wide blue yonder.'

'Yes, and I felt I should make some inquiries or Abe Resznik will think I'm a feeble character. He'll be very worried of course. Sally Walters had the idea that Mr Harland might have heard something?'

Troy's eyes had been suspicious but his expression lightened suddenly. 'That Abe! Some character eh! Needless to say I've heard a lot about him. But I don't think Jerry will have any news for you though he has done some phoning round, chasing up a vague lead. So – you're from London. We were there in 68.' He frowned as he gave the memory some thought. 'Say, is it still raining over there?' he inquired solicitously.

'Not when I left at any rate. Fine and warm in fact. Nearly as hot as it is here today.'

'Really? Jesus, it always seemed to be raining down on us in old London town.' Troy regarded Buchanan silently as he came to a decision. 'Look, I'll close the shop. To hell with the thronging crowds jostling to enter! I'll take you up to meet Jerry. We have our priorities right you see! Friends before business any time.'

Troy moved with a studied grace; apart from the fairy mannerisms there was an indefinable aura of the showbiz world about him. He said: 'You'll get on fine with Jerry. He's a great Anglophile – even talked me into buying one of your tricky little sports cars.' He whistled cheerfully as he locked the front door. He appeared to enjoy the Figaro role of a go-between.

Beyond the inner door the sea-green colour scheme was dropped in favour of a nautical atmosphere with a thick red carpet along a wood-panelled passage, two paintings of yachts, an antique ship's compass and a large brass bell.

Troy negligently pulled open a drawer in a steel cabinet. 'Cones. We tend to specialize in them. Now that's a rarity! A little beauty too.' He pointed to a shell about five inches long with a yellow and brown jagged pattern as if it was made up of shards of pottery. 'The Glory of India cone. Conus milne-edwardsi

Jousseaume. Worth well over a thousand bucks on the collectors' market.' He looked round significantly at Buchanan. 'So – you see – it's quite a big operation we have here. The shop is only the tip of an iceberg. We import, export, sell by mail, supply other dealers . . . '

They had come to a steep flight of wood-panelled stairs with a massive rope strung along one side to act as a banister and contrive the illusion of being on a boat. Troy said: 'We've completely re-modelled our two floors.' He donged the bell and called out: 'Jerry! Jerry! Permission to come aboard? I have a friend of Dave Resznik's with me.'

A door was opened at the top of the stairs and a small figure stood awkwardly in the opening, holding himself braced with a thick cane walking stick. He said 'Yes Troy?' in a tone of faintly tried patience. Behind him there was a background noise of Diana Ross and Motown music.

'Ed Buchanan. A friend of Abe Resznik's – from old London town – and hoping to see Dave.' Buchanan followed Troy up the stairs and into a plainly furnished small office. There were two large steel cabinets of the kind he had seen below, a desk and three chairs. There were neat piles of books on a small table and the desk top looked as if it had just been arranged with geometrical care so that a ruler, pens and pencil formed lines round a blotter. The only decoration on the plain white walls was a framed quotation: 'THE MAN WHO LAUGHS HAS NOT YET BEEN TOLD THE TERRIBLE NEWS – BERT BRECHT'.

Jerry Harland looked about thirty; he had stringy blond hair, an unhealthy complexion and big blue eyes. There was an ambiguity about his innocent gaze. His left leg was stiff and he seemed to accentuate this by the awkward way in which he sat down, as if to say, 'Yes – I'm a cripple – so?' His heavy cane stick had a rubber ferrule and an elaborately carved ivory handle. Some unspoken interrogation was going on between him and Leonard Troy.

Buchanan said: 'Sorry to barge in while you're working but I wondered if you had any news of David. It seems so strange that he went off without saying anything to Mrs Walters or Cherry Kinsella.'

'Ah, so you met Cherry?' Harland spoke in a flat voice. 'Well, Ed, it is just possible that I may hear something later today. Troy – I only just fixed this. I'm taking a run out to Hunters Point – where I may hear – something . . .'

This statement obviously came as a surprise to Troy who made a nervous interjection: 'No. I don't like it – Jerry – not that ratty place.'

'Oh for Chrissake Troy let me decide what *I* shall do. I am not suggesting you should come along.'

'Hunters Point? Where's that?' Buchanan asked. 'Do you think David Resznik may have gone there?'

'Not far. It's part of our fair city but definitely off the tourists' trail. The ugly backside view in fact. No, I don't think Dave is there, but I heard something which makes me want to have a word with someone who lives there.'

'Could I come? Don't hesitate to say no, but I would be interested. I rather like odd-spots in cities.' Buchanan was not sure he was playing his hand right by asking to go along, for he knew that under the hypnosis of suspicion even reasonable responses could sound suspect.

The possibility that this suggestion struck a false note was accentuated by Harland getting up without saying anything and crossing the room to turn off the transistor radio. Troy wore a priestly smile. Harland leant on the table and moved his stiff leg about as if it might be hurting him. 'I don't know,' he said thoughtfully. 'Troy exaggerates the danger of Hunters Point but it is a tough area. Mostly unemployed blacks and whitey isn't particularly welcome there. Not that I'm criticizing. Do you know that Brecht quote: "Who wouldn't rather be polite than rough if only things in general weren't so tough?" ' He sat on the table holding his leg out. Then he smiled in a rather malicious way and imitated a posh British accent: 'Quate shaw you wouldn't prefer to whip orf in yaw Jaguwah to somewhere awf'ly fash'n'ble?'

It was a time to be dull rather than witty. Buchanan replied: 'No Jaguar. No smart plans for this evening and I've done my stint of conventional sightseeing for one day. Hunters Point sounds interesting.'

Harland said 'Okay, okay,' waving some further mumbled

objection from Troy away in a lordly way. 'Don't blow your cool man. So it's a pretty tacky neighbourhood . . .'

'So I don't like the idea of your going there Jer, particularly at this time of day. You know it would be safer in the morning.'

Harland sighed, then spoke peevishly: 'Troy, you know the Great Handicapper has given me a big stone to carry – you!'

Troy raised one last objection in a despairing manner. 'And is it really a good idea to take our Britisher friend along?'

Buchanan longed to say something to cut through all this fairy chatter but managed to stay silent. Harland said: 'One thing's for sure Troy. You always say your piece. It was a nice try but forget it. We're going but we'll be back soon. I don't aim to be there more than a few minutes.'

Troy shrugged. 'So go.'

When Buchanan left the premises of Ocean-Exotica Inc., waving good-bye to Leonard Troy who busied himself with tidying the desk in the shop and removing the parrot's cage, he noticed that the sky had changed dramatically during the previous half-hour. A dense belt of dark cloud was sweeping in from over the Oakland Bay area, so quickly it looked as if a different backcloth was being dragged across a stage. Under the ominously dark clouds he saw another aspect of San Francisco, the dehumanized appearance of its concrete canyons. Buchanan stared at the bleak terrain, grateful for the cool breeze blowing in his face; he welcomed the sudden change in temperature as earlier in the day he had felt rather lethargic and now was just the time when he needed to be thinking quickly – Jerry Harland's face was as impassive as a Japanese tycoon's but Buchanan suspected that it masked a mind sensitive to deceptions.

Harland appeared in a car that shuddered slightly as he applied the brakes. It was a dark green Sunbeam Tiger, the export model with the Mustang 4.7 V8 engine that Buchanan had always liked, an uncomplicated and trouble-free car. Harland had changed his navy pullover and white trousers for a green sweatshirt, faded chinos and field boots. He turned an innocent gaze on Buchanan, smiling slightly, as he started the Tiger and went carelessly through the gears. The engine was missing, and Buchanan felt that the car must often be driven in this manner, without sufficient revving to stop the plugs fouling.

'This is Troy's,' Harland explained, waving his left hand expressively. 'But he don't drive it much. In fact he never gets in it without that clenched-teeth look.' With the change into slumming clothes Harland's manner had become lighter, faintly frivolous, with an air of barely suppressed excitement, like someone who had escaped from an inhibiting background. 'He's very generous about lending it though. Cherry, you met Cherry, she drives it like an angel – a bon-a-roo trip, er, sorry, I mean fantastic! Well, Ed, is this purely a vacation or maybe some business too?'

'Frankly I don't know yet Jerry. I plan to spend a few days seeing the sights and then I'm going to visit my brother who lives in San José. Then I may see some places north of here, the Redwoods, the Humboldt Coast, I've heard it's very beautiful there. Depends on how my money lasts out. And while I'm in the city I may contact some of the car firms on Van Ness, see if there's any chance of a job. Selling cars like this one I mean. British sports jobs. I did quite a bit of driving at one time . . .' He let his statement falter like someone who hopes for quite a lot without much reason to justify optimism.

'Driving? Do you mean racing? Well, that's something!' Harland tried to sound impressed but was not convincing. 'I was going to get you ready for a thumbs-down on your chance of a job here, we're not exactly in the middle of a boom you know, but if you've had racing experience I suppose you stand a chance with one of the firms handling British makes. A racing background and your accent might just swing it.' Harland's gesturing hands had the eloquence of deaf and dumb language. He was obviously more indifferent than suspicious about Buchanan's plans.

'Here, then – you should be able to navigate for me!' He flipped over a map with a blue and white cover lettered 'SAN FRANCISCO Business District One-Way Streets'.

Buchanan studied it with care, showing more interest than he felt, as he would have done if it had been a Chinese dictionary or anything else that might stop a possible interrogation about his relationship with Abe Reznik. On the back it showed a 'Street Plan during BART Construction'.

Harland looked over and raised his eyes in an expression of mock despair. 'You see, Bart is our not-completed, will-it-ever-be-finished, your-guess-is-as-good-as-mine, equivalent of the old Underground in London. What they term the Bay Area Rapid Transit system. We were promised eighty mile an hour speeds, trains at ninety-second intervals, model stations, magnetically coded tickets that actuate passenger gates. You name it, we were to get it. What we have got is absolute chaos and tunnels that don't lead anywhere. Classic case of our shitty capitalist system trying to tackle a public problem . . . Oh well, forget it – I rap on like this at times. I guess I'm feeling nervous – about Dave. I had this funny call. From this guy in Hunters Point who owes me a favour . . . ' He reached up as though to make an adjustment to the driving-mirror, then brushed away an imaginary cobweb from his forehead. 'Yes, you could say I'm feeling nervous.'

'*Could* David be there do you think – in some kind of trouble?'

'I'm quite sure he isn't. Hunters Point isn't a place where you can stay without good friends, and I know Dave doesn't have friends there. That's what puzzles me. Jesus, why should news about Dave reach me from Hunters Point? It's *the* place San Franciscans avoid, like a plague area man! I mean, they may catch a glimpse of it when they're trying for a short-cut to a game at Candlestick Park or hoping to beat the rush-hour traffic on the Bayshore freeway, but that's all. Yes, where we're going is a garbage heap that people like to pretend doesn't exist. Just lately it's become more of a political football and there's a so-called Economic Opportunity Development Programme, but that's about as fake as pre-faded denims. The politicians probably pray each night that it will have vanished in the morning. It's doomsville period.'

As though to illustrate Harland's point, they were travelling through progressively shabbier streets and Buchanan noticed the effect of a narrow shaft of sunlight gilding ugly buildings. Harland was an unusually bad driver who appeared to exult in driving carelessly, as though to demonstrate that it was a purely mechanical skill he did not wish to master. But it was obvious that he did not need a navigator as he threaded his way through a maze of streets without hesitation.

'Fact is, I can tell you more than a little about Hunters Point, Ed. It so happens that, in my idealistic youth, I wrote a short piece about it. You know the kind of thing, socially committed prose with condemning sentences that end up as kind of purple passages, "The still lingering stench of slaughterhouses on Third

Avenue – a heavy truck grinds across to Islais Creek emphasizing the silence of deserted streets and a community without hope." It's an area of "temporary" houses that were put up in a rush for shipyard workers in about 42. In 50 the San Francisco Board of Supervisors endorsed a plan to take over the rundown shacks and replace them with three thousand low-cost housing units. But the plan was postponed, "because of the Korean War", or so they say, and that was the start of twenty years of postponements for dealing with the mess. As the shipyard workers moved out, blacks moved in. It's really a long story, but to put it briefly the black community in this city grew up in three locations. The earliest arrivals were those who came with the railroad, in the old tradition of jobs as porters and waiters; they settled near the Southern Pacific railroad depot. The primary settlement came next in the Fillmore district to feed the needs for servants, maids, semi-skilled jobs. The Hunters Point people came last, didn't fit in so good, and the distinction between the three communities hasn't faded yet. Black people will tell you, for instance, that there are clear differences in dress, style and attitude between residents of the Western Addition and those in the Hunters Point ghetto. Unemployment among the younger men in Hunters Point has been as high as fifty-three per cent in recent times. With a situation like that, how can you expect anything but trouble? Jesus . . . ' Harland paused, mentally dealing with some uncomfortable thought; he was having trouble with an invisible cobweb again. 'I just remembered, the bims, the cops, shot a black boy there just about a week ago.' He turned towards Buchanan with an unhappy grin. 'If you should want out we'll turn right around and I'll make the trip tomorrow morning. It'll sound absurd to you, but it might be safer then.'

'Don't turn round for me,' Buchanan said flatly, determined not to give Harland any excuse for changing his plan. 'I'm for black people, not against them. My favourite place to eat in London is a Jamaican restaurant called Ochos Rios – I travel right across London from east to west to get there, mainly because I enjoy their humour and liveliness. I don't like the idea of accepting a situation of being afraid of going into a black community, as if it was a lions' den.'

64

Harland smiled bleakly. 'Man, this isn't like going to your favourite restaurant. These people don't give a shit about whether you're prejudiced or not. Fact is, I just plain forgot about that boy Clarence Johnson being killed and it's liable to have made them jumpy . . . ' He debated the point with himself for a moment, then said: 'Okay, okay, but I wish I was stoned. Still, the bit about Clarence Johnson was the bad news. The good news is that the place I'm going to visit is right on the edge of the area. The plan is – we park in Hunters Point Boulevard. I run up the slope . . . ' He made a humorous expression to underline the impossibility of this idea. 'With a little luck I'll only need a few minutes to make my contact. Then maybe the pro driver will take over and whip us out. Say Ed, how do you feel about a steak when this is all over? We could go to Lew Lehr's on Steiner – you choose your steak, fillay or whatever, say how much – he makes a price for the meat and that's the price of your dinner. I think you'd enjoy it. And maybe a few beers?'

Buchanan pounced on the suggestion with enthusiasm. He was tired of his own dishonest attempts to sound honest. 'Fine. I had a marvellous stew at Sally Walters's house at lunchtime but in an hour or so, yes, a steak would go down well. I wanted to ask you, Jerry, you seem to know so much about Hunters Point – you must have some kind of sociological interest in the place?'

Harland nodded ponderously. When he replied his tone was free from nervousness, slightly self-important. 'You could say that. Yes, I do have an interest in radical politics, but simply in trying to help the people. Troy too – he's part of the radical tradition of this state . . . ' He turned to look searchingly at Buchanan. 'You – you didn't recognize him did you?'

'No. What do you mean? Should I have?'

'Never seen him? No, oh well, there you are – poor old Troy always expects . . . He used to be in movies, you see. In the forties and early fifties. The name Richard Troy doesn't ring a bell? No? Well they were mostly B movies, cowboy pix from Republic. Fillums in which the directors' only interest was "who are the guys who wear the white hats and who are the guys who wear the black hats?" Troy was 4F and didn't get into the services, so he was available and he had quite a vogue for a few years. Then

· 5

they dropped him. But he'd saved his loot. He'd always been keen on the sea, collected shells, sailed a yacht. So then he made a hobby into business. Took a small shop on Bush and bought a house by Stinson Beach – that's across the Golden Gate Bridge, near Mount Tamalpais. He's still got it since he prefers to live in Cabbageville. Anyway Troy's background is pure Hollywood, the son of a cameraman and a bit-part player, born in a house on the corner of Yucca and Grace, only a short walk from Hollywood Boulevard. He's been a radical ever since high school. You see, in the thirties the Ku Klux Klan spawned lots of fascist organizations like the Black Legion, Father Coxey's Blue Shirts, the American White Guard. Probably the largest and most fantasy-ridden of the groups formed on the Nazi model was right here in California, William Dudley Pelley's Silver Legion. Pelley had been a scenario writer for cowboy pix. Somebody had to make a stand against them. Troy did that.'

Something about this seemingly simple concluding statement struck a false note. It sounded paranoiac to Buchanan and he could only murmur 'I see. Yes,' as he had done at intervals throughout the monologue. The vision of Leonard Troy alone opposing the forces of fascism was ridiculous; it was the vast majority of people in America who had the good sense to resist the rhetoric of demagogues like Pelley and Huey Long.

Harland said: 'We're on Third Street now, running parallel with the waterfront. We cross the Islais Creek Channel and then make a left on to Hunters Point Boulevard. Won't be long now.' He used both hands to make an inconclusive gesture, then relapsed into thoughtful silence.

Buchanan stared at the vast industrial slum they were traversing. The land looked as if it had been systematically laid waste: there were acres of desolation and it was hard to believe that so much ugliness could have been contrived quite accidentally by foundering businesses. The procession of closed-down workshops and empty yards bounded by rusting wire fences seemed unending. There was a pervasive, acrid smell of burning rubber. The colours were of concrete and metal.

'A good place to nurture grievances, eh?' Harland asked, shaking his head from side to side. 'I mean you're a black kid so the dice are loaded against you anyway, you're living in a beat-up shack in Quint Street or on Palou Avenue, your education's a bad joke, you're unemployed with no prospect of finding work, and finally you're surrounded by this . . . This . . . ' He gave up searching for a suitably descriptive phrase. When he started to talk again his tone became lighter. 'I tell you, Ed, your favourite restaurant may be a Jamaican place and you may get on well with West Indians, but you'll find it hard to make friends with the blacks here. For a start they don't want your friendship, then they've got this parlance, a slang talk that's hard to follow. There are bewildering alternatives for money for instance – that can be bread, cake, jack, dust or wine. A woman can be a mink, bat, stallion, snag or leg.'

Buchanan shook his head. 'I promise – I shan't be starting any conversations. I shall just try to fade into the background.'

'Okay, okay. You see I don't fancy ending up sounding more nervous than Troy, and you look as if you can handle yourself, but it could be a bad scene with this Clarence Johnson situation . . . And then there are the hypers, dopers. Look, see that Bogart-type saloon!'

They had been travelling along deserted streets as if in a ghost-town, and the big black Buick approaching them was the first car they had seen in five minutes. Eight black people were crammed into the car, all vividly dressed and in an exuberant mood. The windows were wound down and the radio was blaring out music with a strong rocking beat. The expression of the driver changed to one of bitterness as he passed the Tiger, and he called out something and clenched a big fist.

Harland murmured 'And screw you!' then sighed and said 'Looks like there's been a wedding.'

Buchanan asked 'That's good news?': it was a mischievous question as he already knew the answer from Harland's tone.

Harland looked at him with childish candour. 'What do you think? With a wedding here there's always non-stop drinking. Oh well, shit, this has got to work! Kindly observe Hunters Point Boulevard.'

They were passing a particularly desolate scene, a vast area filled with disintegrating cars and the eloquent hoarding LAST

MILE AUTO WRECKERS. There were some wooden shacks and on their left hand side, nearest to the Bay, a row of boarded-up shops. 'Big Daddy's Soul Food Café' looked as if it had been hit by a riot and then abandoned. On the right side of the road there was a steep dust slope that might have been a tidied-up rubbish heap but for a few flat-topped houses perched on the edge of the summit.

Harland braked suddenly, as was his wont, saying 'Yes, suh, here we am!'

'I'll come up there with you. Hover around at the top, then I can keep an eye on the Tiger and – be on hand . . .'

Harland gave Buchanan a mistrustful sidelong look, showing for the first time a hint of suspicion. 'You really want to come? Say, you sound as if you welcome trouble.' He shrugged again. 'Oh well, it's just not my bag I guess – this kind of scene. My number one priority group? Me. Okay, come on then.'

The steep concrete path up the dust slope was covered with graffiti in paint and coloured chalks. A sentence which started off 'When the eagle flies' ended up in graphic sexual boasting. There were drawings of a dwarf burdened with enormous genitals and a thin man with a penis longer than his leg. There was a strong smell of rubbish and urine. Harland stopped to bend forward awkwardly, examining something on the path like Sherlock Holmes. 'Yep. See that snake-head confetti and those conical wads of cotton-candy paper? There's been a wedding here all right. Don't come any further. Keep an eye on Troy's auto – I'd like to take it back reasonably intact if possible.' He walked off as briskly as he could, swinging his heavy cane.

The rows of small houses looked like a service camp left over from the Second World War and there were no signs of life. In the nearest house the windows were all covered with tobacco-coloured curtains.

Under the dark clouds there was an overwhelming air of oppressiveness about Hunters Point. Buchanan wasn't intimidated by the 'Kill Whitey' sign in oxblood red paint that lay practically below his feet, but he was sensitive to the intolerable living conditions that surrounded him – he felt that the slum area was like a gigantic festering boil that urgently needed to be lanced.

Looking along the lines of flat roofs, he thought about David Resznik who might be hiding there. He was experiencing more sympathy and fellow feeling for Resznik than he would have believed possible when he had embarked on the flight to San Francisco. He saw a rough parallel between Resznik's position and his own, in that they had both become involved gradually in situations they could not handle. He had started what he thought would be a light-hearted affair with an unattached woman and found himself emotionally tangled-up with Mrs Laura Mayhew whose husband was dying from leukaemia.

There was no doubt that Laura was, sexually, the most exciting woman he had ever met. She could induce a feeling of giddy exaltation in him with the warmth of her kisses, the urgency of her caresses and the excitement of her total capitulation 'as if there was no tomorrow'. Physically she still captivated him; the pearly sheen of her back, the shape of her arms, the smell of her neck – making love to her was like falling into bottomless water. But if he could cope with her sexual demands he was inadequate when it came to all the emotional upheavals, the tears, the wild fits of jealousy and anger. Finally, he was not willing to have a relationship with a woman who was betraying a dying husband. So an intolerable situation had developed.

He could visualize how a comparable dilemma had developed with David Resznik. The brilliant young Trotskyite, author of inflammatory widely-published articles, grandson of the legendary revolutionary, would have undoubtedly found a rapturous welcome among the wild radicals of the Berkeley campus. From that position it would have been easy for him to become gradually involved with some plan for direct action, the final developments of which he did not approve. There was a chasm between the theoretical advocation of violence and actually taking part in an assassination.

Bound up in his thoughts Buchanan was walking to and fro like a sentry, from the shack with the curtained windows to the point where he had the Tiger in view. Now he paused as he dealt

69

with the heart of the matter. Basically did not the trouble lie in his own character and that of David R.? They were both *posing* instead of being. Since witnessing his mother's excruciating death in the place they had called an Intensive Care Unit, but which resembled a torture chamber, he had looked on the world in a different light – seeing the cruelty and chaos which lay beneath the surface appearance. He knew this had affected his feelings – perhaps he was 'not capable of real love', 'cold', 'a cool bastard with cold-looking eyes' – all the phrases that Laura had thrown at him were possibly true. And in Resznik's case maybe he just lacked the guts to carry out policies he had so often advocated.

'Hey Mickey Mouse!' 'Lookit, the Man!' At the bottom of the concrete path three Negroes were calling up to him. 'Hey honky!' 'What you doin' there man? – this private property, grey boy!'

Two of the Negroes were of medium height, but they flanked a giant who would top Buchanan's own six feet two by another three or four inches. The giant was dressed in white overalls of the kind used by garage employees, while the smaller men wore light gaberdine suits and jazzy ties. Buchanan knew trouble when he saw it: he had got his knowledge the hard way, and he saw it written plainly in the giant's face, his rolling eyeballs and spastic shoulder movements. While his companions continued to call out contemptuous comments, largely requests of an impossible anatomical nature, the big man, who had the name 'Duke' in red letters over his breast pocket, was ominously silent.

When he was a few yards from Buchanan, Duke spoke for the first time: the words came out rather jumbled-up as if released under pressure. 'Paddy . . . you . . . hangin' round my main squeeze?'

Buchanan wanted to avoid trouble if it was possible. His instructions before leaving England had been explicit on that point, stressing the tricky nature of his undercover investigations relating to David Resznik: he was supposed to do a tightrope walk, gathering information but not becoming involved in any police matters. His response to Duke was soft-spoken, as if he had to apologize for living: 'Just waiting for a friend. We shall be gone in a few minutes.'

Now that they were closer the two smaller men hung back,

eyeing Buchanan with something akin to respect, sensing danger in his powerfully built body and unusually wide shoulders. They waited to see if Duke was going to make the action. One of them said quietly 'Don't blow your cool man,' but Duke wasn't receptive to advice. He uttered a few incomprehensible words and threw a haymaking left.

With this first wild punch, Buchanan realized that Duke was drunk and that he had misread a drunken gait for uncontrollable fury. The most lethal thing about Duke was his breath, a potent mixture of raw onion and beer which smelt like carbide in water. Duke boxed according to the *Carmen Jones* manual: 'Stand toe to toe, trade blow for blow'. He was a southpaw who held his right arm in front of him like a massive club. Buchanan knew he could drop him any time he felt inclined, but he wanted to bring the fight to a halt with the minimum of injury and hard feeling. Duke's well-signalled blows came over with so much force that it was like dodging falling tree-trunks. Buchanan held both hands high to protect himself but concentrated on bobbing and weaving, making the giant look hopelessly ponderous and clumsy. One particularly massive blow took Duke off-balance; he stumbled and would have fallen but Buchanan held him up in a clinch, saying 'I could have danced all night.'

Duke shot him a surprised look as if seeing him for the first time, then said 'Yes, baby, we're waltzing.' The admission seemed to release his pent-up feelings of aggression as he dropped his arms and burst out laughing.

One of the smaller men said to Buchanan: 'You played that game before, man.' Buchanan rubbed the top of his ear which had been seared by one of Duke's punches, saying 'It's not a game I like particularly. What I would like is to wait here just a few more minutes, minding my own business, and then be off.' He pointed down the path to the Tiger.

The other small man asked: 'You British?' Buchanan nodded, then said 'London Scottish.' It was one of his father's stock replies when asked if he was Scots, an absurdly inappropriate statement to a Negro in Hunters Point but it appeared to go down quite well as all three black men began to nod and shrug at the same time. Duke pretended to throw one last punch, saying 'So

71

we'll be back, Paddy, in about twenty minutes. Be gone then.' He shambled off, followed by his friends like a champion going back to his dressing-room.

Buchanan's face stung and he realized that another of Duke's blows must have been closer than he had judged in the excitement of the fight. The evening breeze was fresh and would soon cool his inflamed cheek. He looked up, seeing it was what his mother would have called a curds-and-whey sky. A sound on the concrete path made him wheel round, ready for more trouble, and it was a relief to hear Harland's cane and laboured steps.

When Harland appeared his face was white and strained. He walked straight past Buchanan, saying 'Keep moving, Ed. We'll split. Right now.'

'Any news about David?'

'Yep, he was here all right. Someone saw him and Fred Wheeler – he's Dave's closest pal – on Earl Street just a week ago. Jesus, this is bad news, Ed. I mean, you know, really terrible. The guy I saw said they were with two mean, bad guys. You should see the guy who told me that – like if he says "mean, bad" . . . '

'What can we do? Could you go to the police?'

Harland stopped walking for a moment, staring at Buchanan, shaking his head. For a moment he appeared to hover on the point of making some real confidence, then changed his mind. 'What could I tell them? This guy who told me would just deny – everything. And the cops wouldn't get it from him with thumbscrews. No, I've got to find Fred Wheeler. They were seen here, in Earl Street, last Tuesday. I know Fred's surfaced in the Haight since then.' He paused wearily in the awkward downhill walk. 'Jesus, I'm sick and tired of trouble. This is driving me out of my skull. You fool, Dave, you fool.'

II

Buchanan woke from a dream of chasing a dust phantom over a great heap of ashes in which his feet sank ever more deeply. He was amused by this simple stratagem of his unconscious and said, 'Thank you, Dr Freud,' then tried to remember the part of his dream before the chase began. He felt it also related to his search for David Resznik, a portentous memory that tantalizingly refused to be changed into anything recognizable. Glancing at his watch on the bedside table he saw that it was only 5 a.m. – too early to get up, yet he doubted whether he could get back to sleep and possibly confront the phantom.

In his racing days Buchanan had often resorted to his own equivalent of counting sheep – doing a mental lap round the Brands Hatch track. Mechanically he began the circuit without much hope that it still had a drowsy magic for him. He built up the revs to 10,000 then slipped into second and, moments later, third, with a touch on the brakes at the tricky Paddock Hill bend, cutting across the apex and swooping down the hill and up to Druids Bend. Braking hard and changing down into second, pulling her round as fast as she would go without sliding, then up again into third, snatching fourth for a few seconds and back into third for the notoriously tricky left-hand sweep. Breasting the hill to reach the fastest part of the circuit, up to fourth and fifth, hitting more than 150 m.p.h. before taking Hawthorn's Bend . . .

Buchanan laughed at himself. He could do fifty complete laps and be no nearer sleep. The warning hidden within his dream was still teasing him. He got out of bed and looked down from the window at the rather shabby shops and garages that made up the less fashionable end of Post Street. Now that he was better orientated he knew that he was looking in the direction of

Chinatown which had seemed like an oasis of sanity after the hours spent with Jerry Harland in the Haight-Ashbury and North Beach areas, fruitlessly searching for Fred Wheeler.

The wild goose chase, particularly on Broadway, had made him realize that there was a surprising puritanical streak in his own nature. The commercialized obsession with sex in that area, like a lewd fairground with a succession of leering neon signs – CHEAP THRILLS: TOTALLY NUDE COLLEGE CO-EDS: NUDE LIVE FLESH: SEX SHOW: HE & SHE LOVE IN – had become claustrophobic. This had probably been exaggerated because he had felt quite superfluous in the search, sitting around in bars while Harland chatted up the *habitués*. The sole positive result of hours spent in 'Big Al's', 'Roaring 20s' and the 'Hungry I' was a confirmation that Fred Wheeler had been seen on several occasions since the date when he had gone with David Resznik to Hunters Point. Jerry Harland had appeared to be cheered by this, but after so much drinking it was hard to tell how much of his optimism came from all the beer and whisky they had downed.

'A man may escape from his enemies, or even his friends, but how shall a man escape from his own nature?' Buchanan had remembered this quotation for years though he had long forgotten the author, and it had become part of his often-used mental furniture, like his father's phrases of potted wisdom. Suddenly he realized that his dream had been linked in some way with it and that he had been momentarily aware of imminent danger bound up in an aspect of his own nature which he could not change.

Once the puzzle was solved it seemed of no consequence. Buchanan got back into bed and picked up a copy of *California Living* which he had found in the wardrobe, and began to read an article headed 'Understanding Twentieth Street'. Almost immediately he fell into a dreamless sleep for what seemed only a minute, but when he opened his eyes sunlight was streaming into the room and it was 8.30.

As he shaved and showered, Buchanan was brooding on Sally Walters's house in Laguna Street. Thinking of that happy, sane household was an effective antidote to the sordid images of North Beach. It was obvious from the house, its furnishings, and Sally

Walters' style of living that she must have been left quite well-off when her husband died and did not need to take in lodgers. It would appear that she let some of the rooms simply because she enjoyed the company of younger people. When he had lunched there Buchanan had become aware of this, and that David Resznik was regarded as being 'one of the family' which made him experience a fleeting feeling of envy.

The telephone rang while Buchanan was still in the shower and he answered it holding a towel round his waist. 'Mr Bu-chan-an! A call for you Mr Bu-chan-an.' The voice of the Chinese girl on the hotel switchboard sounded very young and pleasant. He thanked her and waited for a moment while some coughing took place at the other end of the line, then a deep masculine voice asserted itself: 'That you, Buchanan?'

'Yes.'

The deep voice became slightly self-conscious: 'Vraiment Monsieur Quelquechose?'

'Oui. Monsieur Autrechose?'

'Good. I shall want to see you this morning. First thing. Got anything for me?'

'Yes. I was going to phone you a little later. I would have done last night but I didn't get back here till 2.45.'

'That's all right. Fine, so we both have something. Look, we'll make it in the Golden Gate Park. Nice place for a quiet chat. Neutral ground and perhaps we'll pop into the Steinhart Aquarium. Place I want to visit anyway. Kill two birds. Nearly nine now, time for breakfast, etcetera. Make it ten ack emma. Get your hotel to order a taxi and tell him to drop you, let's think a moment, yes, on the corner of Fulton Street and Arguello Boulevard. That's at the north boundary of the park. Then walk straight into the park, along what's called the Conservatory drive, double back on your tracks a bit so you get the tennis courts and lily-pond on your left hand and stroll along the Middle drive, following the signs to the aquarium. Till *I* contact *you*. *I'll* make myself known. Understood?' Jack Collier's voice had a sharp edge to it, as if he was in a testy mood.

'Understood. Walking along Middle drive at ten o'clock.'

'See you.' The line went dead.

As he dressed and breakfasted, Buchanan was marshalling the information he had for Collier. There was only one tangible piece of evidence, Resznik's diary, but that could well prove to be important when brought together with other facts. And he had built up quite a picture of Resznik's life in California, considering that he had only been actively concerned with it for twenty-four hours.

By the time he was in a cab driven by an amiable-looking but silent Negro, Buchanan felt that he had got his facts and theories about David Resznik in reasonable order. He was hoping that Collier would allow the undercover approach to continue as he felt this was likely to prove more effective than an official probing. Certainly Harland had said that his informant in Hunters Point could not be made to talk 'with thumbscrews'.

The yellow cab was speeding across the city from east to west, making good speed on Geary Boulevard which Sally Walters told him had been named after Colonel John W. Geary, who became the first mayor of San Francisco in 1850. The city looked clean and white in the sunlight, and his memories of Hunters Point seemed like grotesque incidents in his dream.

Buchanan followed a crocodile of school children into the Golden Gate Park. As soon as he found Middle drive he saw Jack Collier waiting on a seat, reading a newspaper and with a pile of others by his side. Collier wore a ginger and blue check sports-coat with grey cord trousers, a white shirt and a striped tie. He looked very fit, like a professional golfer. He patted the seat to indicate that Buchanan could sit down.

'On the dot.' He watched the children till they were out of sight, then placed the paper he had been reading with the others and got out his pipe and a pouch of tobacco. 'Read any good books lately?'

Buchanan was slightly bewildered by this banality and began to wonder if he was in for another public exchange of information like the one they had on the plane from London. He had only read two books in the last twelve months, and had forgotten everything about *The Leopard* apart from its ironic ending. '*The Caine Mutiny*. About the U.S. Navy during the war.'

'I know it.' Collier nodded several times. 'Very good book, that.

Factual background. Kind of thing I like. I've got this large appetite for facts, you see. You could reel off a hundred facts about Resznik junior, for instance, from weight at birth to present collar size, and I wouldn't be bored.'

Buchanan did not smoke but he was interested to watch the way in which Collier filled his pipe and lit it. A workmanlike performance, an unhurried ritual which the blunt fingers carried out like a machine independent of the man who owned the 'bird's-eye' grain briar and the yellow tobacco pouch. Collier concentrated in silence on the pipe as he got it alight, the muscles of his face and neck working slightly. When the dry, bittersweet aroma of the smoke began to rise he blinked a few times, and this too seemed part of a ritual. There was something about Collier's steady character that was attractive and he was obviously a good man to have on one's side.

After a minute or two of silent smoking Collier put a proprietary hand on the top paper, the *San Francisco Chronicle*. 'You didn't see this I suppose? Yesterday's issue. Young Resznik's dead.'

'What! And in the papers! But I saw Mrs Walters, where he lived, and three of his friends yesterday and none of them knew about it . . . '

'They wouldn't, laddie. No way of knowing.' Collier took the top paper and folded it carefully before handing it to Buchanan. 'It's that short piece, with the headline "Faceless man found at Fort Point". There was no clue as to identity on the body you see. And it was found bundled up in a tarpaulin that had been used to cover cement. When they pulled the tarpaulin off most of the face came with it. I've seen a few stiffs but this is a gruesome one, believe me. No laundry marks on his shirt that could be traced either. Funny. There I was at the British Consulate conferring with the security people about the absent David R. and in waltz two men from the Homicide Department asking if the Consulate had a record of any British citizens who had gone missing lately. It was like, what's that game? The card game for children where you have two packs of identical cards that have to be matched? – yes, Snap.'

Buchanan could not accept the news of David Resznik's death

equably like Collier. He was thinking of its effect on the Walters family. One image from Resznik's room there, the two pairs of tennis shoes lying by the wardrobe, floated into his mind. He blotted out this melancholy, pointless thought and asked: 'How come? I mean, why should the Homicide men arrive at the Consulate if there was nothing to identify Resznik?'

'Well, there were some Marks & Spencer brand labels in his pants and socks. And he had a lot of fillings in his teeth which their forensic people thought were European. Last evening, acting together, we clinched the matter. Tracked down the dentist Resznik went to in Berkeley. He was able to give us a positive identification. The dental record in his file matched exactly. The poor dentist chappy was even able to point out a crown and two fillings he had done himself. Not a pleasant way to spend ten minutes I must say. He looked very green by the time it was over. So David Resznik is undoubtedly dead, the subject of a San Francisco Police Department Incident Form, No. 27365, all six copies filled out by Sergeant Pickering. No one's to be told about this for the time being of course. I can tell you that when the police here got the picture they were very unhappy. The idea of this young revolutionary running into our place on Montgomery Street babbling something about a plot getting out of control, then being allowed to run out again. You can imagine their re-action. And I had to add fuel to the fire by telling them that Resznik was a name we'd been rather fond of for some time – had to let them know about the grandfather's record. Well, we can't rectify past mistakes but Resznik's pals in the plot have got to be found fastish . . .'

'I spent all yesterday evening with one of Resznik's friends, a man called Jerry Harland. He's the assistant, and I suspect the boyfriend, of a Mr Leonard Troy who owns a shop selling exotic sea-shells . . .'

'Hold on a minute. I'll take a note of this.' Jack Collier produced his tiny notebook and a gold propelling pencil.

'The shop is called Ocean-Exotica Inc., on the corner of Polk and Geary Avenues. Both men are undoubtedly close friends of Resznik, but my feeling is they are unlikely to be involved directly in the plot or whatever. Yesterday evening I went with Harland to a place called Hunters Point, a kind of black ghetto area to the south, by the naval dockyard. An acquaintance of Harland's told him that Resznik had been seen there on the 5th, the day after he visited the Consulate. With another friend named Fred Wheeler . . .'

'Wait. That's a name already in my notes. The police in Berkeley had it as being linked with Resznik's. They organized a couple of demonstrations some months ago, protest meetings which turned violent. And he's got a long civil disobedience record too, probably ripe for some real roguery. Have you got the Negro's name – the one in Hunters Point?'

'No, nor the address. I only got to go along with Harland by not pressing anything, appearing concerned about Resznik but not *too* interested, so when Harland said wait at the edge of the area I did just that. All his informant was willing to say was that Resznik and Wheeler had been seen in Earl Street "with two mean, bad guys" . . .'

'Were they, by God! That's important, Buchanan. You see, the Homicide people here feel the m.o. of the killing points to it being a professional job, what they call a "hit". The fact that he was slugged to death with a large Colt revolver and, particularly, the disposal of the body. Apparently the evidence points to it having been carted along a rather select residential street just at the edge of the Presidio, a large military establishment with its own hospital, airfield and an old fort. Then they must have dumped the corpse in the sea close to the fort, just under the Golden Gate Bridge. Logical enough in a way as there are very few places here with direct access to deep water, but it would take know-how and lots of nerve. Well, anyway, that's how the Homicide people see it. They don't think a murderous quarrel between Resznik and his revolutionary chums would have ended up like that.'

'Do you want me to try for more information? If the police pull Harland in for questioning everything may get jammed up.'

'We'll see. Now this has become a murder case our position here is even trickier. But Lieutenant Green seems a reasonable man, probably he'll agree we might get more by you sneaking in the side entrance rather than by battering down the front door.

79

As soon as we've finished our chat, you go back to the Jerome. I'll ring you by lunch time. Anything else for me?'

'Yes. I borrowed David Resznik's diary, lifted it from his room in Mrs Walters's house.' Buchanan handed it to Collier who raised his eyebrows at the sight of the small blue pages. 'Not very much in it. A resumé of the political scene here on the pages at the front. Apart from that there are only dates, place names and figures, but they might add up to a kind of key.'

Collier's eyes gleamed. 'Your journey *was* necessary. Yes, I think we can safely say we didn't waste taxpayers' cash in buying your air ticket. Homicide have got a page from that very diary tucked away in Room 450 of the Hall of Justice on Bryant Street. They found it with a photograph and a few dollar bills in a wallet on the body. Now, if you can just tell me the special significance of the word quicksilver the mystery may be solved.'

'Means nothing to me. Quicksilver, mercury, nothing.'

'It appears to have puzzled Resznik too. On that torn-out diary page he'd written down place names again and numbers too, along with Fred Wheeler's initials, and then the word quicksilver, followed by its dictionary definition, as if he was trying to find some hidden meaning in it. Any more treasures concealed about you?'

'No. I met Resznik's girl friend, an Anglo-Irish girl called Cherry Kinsella – she boards at the same house in Laguna Street. But I only saw her for a minute, just said hello.'

'Right then.' Collier flipped quickly through the diary. 'We've done well I think. Look, I want to ask you something but we'll have a quick stroll through the aquarium. Won't get another chance. Whatever happens here I want you to fly back to London within the next forty-eight hours to keep a watch on Abe Resznik and his young pals. Somehow I feel this affair will link up with him.'

Collier stood up and knocked out his pipe on his heel, then leant forward to riffle the pile of papers on the park bench. There were copies of *New Morning*, *Workers Vanguard*, *Pamoja Venceremos*, *Desafio*, *Berkeley Barb* and others Buchanan had seen scattered about Resznik's room. Collier grunted and made a non-committal gesture above them, saying, 'Required reading for me at the moment. Half-baked stuff a lot of it, but at least they express some ideals. What I can't stomach are their so-called "comics". I just don't understand why this revolutionary stuff should go hand-in-hand with a craving for drugs, perverted sex and filth like those comics. My God but there must be a lot of mighty sick people in this town, Buchanan! Believe me, their world is so depraved that smashing in someone's head like an egg must seem pretty normal behaviour.'

As they walked along the path to the large building which housed the Steinhart Aquarium, the Morrison Planetarium and the African Hall, Buchanan was still digesting the fact of David Resznik's death. The event had been conveyed in three words, a terse phrase to describe the brutish termination of a human existence. To Buchanan it seemed another demonstration of the essential absurdity of human lives in a world governed by caprice. One day Resznik would have been working in his room in Mrs Walters's house, a brilliant young intellectual with a coterie of friends and admiring readers; a few days later he was being battered to death and disposed of like rubbish. He conjured up Jerry Harland's blank onanistic face, and the anxious visage of Leonard Troy, fighting a losing battle against age, with a faint moustache of nervous perspiration. If they were somehow involved in Resznik's plot there would be scant satisfaction in knowing they had been brought to justice. But the mysterious 'two mean, bad guys', ah, that was a different matter. There was an irresistible allure about them.

Two Japanese youths were standing on the steps near the building, engaged in trying to sell hydrogen-filled balloons, but there was no one else in sight. Collier said: 'I'll get these. See you on the ice,' and hurried forward to purchase the tickets. His tone was paternalistic and slightly patronizing, probably due to his superior rank. Communication with him, at anything but a superficial level, would be difficult.

Once in the large foyer, staring down at alligators so steadfastly immobile that it was difficult to know if they were real, Buchanan could hear the muffled noise of distant voices and laughter, but they were alone as they made their way along the dimly lit corridors. Collier walked at a steady pace, giving the inmates of each tank a short intense stare. He brought the inspection to a halt by the tank containing electric eels, with an oscilloscope mounted by it on which it was possible to see a 600-volt discharge. He looked both ways, with the first hint of a cloak-and-dagger manner, then said: 'Well laddie, you're the Resznik expert. Can you give me an explanation for his very odd behaviour. I mean at the Consulate.'

'Perhaps. I think I can understand it. All his "direct action" was theoretical, just words on paper . . .'

'The best crimes are committed in the brain,' Collier suggested.

'Yes. He doesn't seem to have taken part in anything in Britain. No police record at any rate. But here he finds himself tied in with a wild bunch who really mean it. They want to go to the limit. Or perhaps he sees, he's very bright, that their plan is stupid, that people may be killed and nothing worthwhile achieved. So he goes to the Consulate because he can't think of another way of stopping whatever it is or was, but once there he realizes that his evidence will be used against his friends. They'll end up in prison.'

'All right. Fair enough. Panicking is the short explanation. He panics about the plot, then he panics about giving it away. But if so, why the heavy mob? If so, why does he have to be *killed*?'

'No idea. But I hope Lieutenant Green will let me try for more information.'

'If he does, remember we've no official status here. Keep out of trouble. If something tricky is going to develop, back away – understand that?' Collier looked at Buchanan closely. 'You seem keen on this job.'

Buchanan adopted a suitably offhand tone. 'Just want to follow it through.'

12

SMILE, BE CRUEL

HUMANITY WON'T BE HAPPY UNTIL THE LAST
BUREAUCRAT IS HUNG WITH THE GUTS OF THE
LAST CAPITALIST!

COMRADES! IT'S *YOUR* TURN TO PLAY! *TOGETHER*
WE CAN CREATE REVOLUTIONARY SITUATIONS

THE URGE TO DESTROY IS REALLY A CREATIVE URGE!

The placards in the small shop window added up to a crude
re-statement of David Resznik's views. Ostensibly a bookshop,
there was little on display that appeared to be for sale and it was
dominated by enormous photographs of 'François Koenigstein,
known as Jules Ravachol. Born 11 October 1854. Reasons for
detention: destruction of buildings and possession of bombs' and
'Nestor Makhno, Russian peasant revolutionary, whose insurgent
army of the Ukraine fought against all the enemies of the revolu-
tion – Bolsheviks, liberals and Czarists'. Jerry Harland had
included the shop in his futile search for Fred Wheeler that had
occupied much of the Tuesday evening, and on Wednesday
13 October Buchanan made it his last place of call in duplicat-
ing the search. Apart from a thin-faced dark girl the shop was
empty. Buchanan turned away and walked round the corner from
Filbert Street into Stockton which he knew would take him
back through Chinatown in the general direction of his hotel.

It was 7.30 p.m. and Buchanan was feeling hungry, hot and
tired. He had not eaten anything since breakfast and he was
looking forward to a shower, changing his clothes, and a steak

and salad dinner. After the lunch-time telephone message from Jack Collier had given him the go-ahead to continue his under-cover inquiries, he had spent a useless frustrating six hours. His phone call to the Ocean-Exotica premises had not been answered, and when he had visited the shop he found the 'Closed' sign hanging on the door. His only real chance of achieving anything had been whisked away like the parrot's cage, and he had mooched around, following the previous evening's trail, with the vague hope of spotting Wheeler.

Walking around Washington Square Buchanan admitted to himself that he was probably beaten. If Troy and Harland had left the city on business and were to stay away for only a day or two, or if they had gone off on a trip to Baja California which Harland had described as being 'our favourite place', then his chances of obtaining more information were negligible. In forty-eight hours he would be back in London. He did not like being beaten, there was something of his father's bulldog tenacity in his own character, but there came a point where it had to be accepted. He resolved to forget the David Resznik affair for a while and enjoy what was probably his last evening in San Francisco.

On the corner of Pacific Avenue Buchanan stared up at the sky. The mad momentum of the city's daytime traffic had notice-ably slackened. It was a calm still evening and the setting sun had painted the sky a glorious wash ranging from cerise to gold. The orange sun was reflected in thousands of windows, while lights were coming on all over the city to illuminate skyscrapers, spires and domes like an enormous firework set-piece. There was only a handful of lavender clouds, shaped like boats and islands, touched with the colour of pomegranate seeds along one edge. It was a beautiful world and one should be able to be happy in it.

Strolling slowly through Chinatown, staring in shop windows at displays of jade and ivory and then at the unusual vegetables outside a greengrocers, Buchanan thought of asking Mrs Sally Walters to have dinner with him. It would be reasonable to return her hospitality and very enjoyable to share a meal with her, either a modest one in a Chinese place or splurging some money at the Hotel Mark Hopkins at the top of Nob Hill. The idea was like a house of cards which was carefully built up but demolished in a second by thinking of how unpleasant it would be to act a part with her now that he knew David Resznik was dead.

By the time he could see the modest sign of the Hotel Jerome Buchanan had become reconciled to a lonely evening, but the prospect of more hours of only his own company recalled tantalizing memories of times spent with Laura Mayhew. Images and thoughts jostled for expression: a weakness about her mouth and chin coupled with the asseveration of someone determined to have her own way; her saying, 'Simply mad about the boy' and 'I love you – ' followed by a tiny pause as though she had forgotten exactly who it was she loved; the movement of her breasts as she threw back her arms; the warmth of her kisses. It was quite simple – he wanted the best of both worlds – the sexual excitement of Mrs Laura Mayhew combined with the stability and domesticity of Mrs Sally Walters.

The foyer of the Hotel Jerome was crowded, and with a brief nod a young Chinese girl behind the reception desk handed him his key and a folded sheet of paper. It was a quarto sheet of yellow paper with two sentences written in the middle in jet black ink. A felt pen and innate artistry had combined to make it look like an entry in a calligraphic competition. '18.00 hours – Miss Kinsella phoned. 19.00 hours – Miss Kinsella phoned.'

As Buchanan made his way to the lift studying this enigmatic message he heard his name being called in a rich, clipped voice, the kind suitable for delivering withering remarks. He turned to see Cherry Kinsella standing by the entrance. There was a smile on her pale face but it was wan and uncertain. She looked nervous and preoccupied. He hurried over to her, crumpling the yellow paper.

'They told you I phoned you? Are you going out this evening?' Cherry Kinsella asked these questions without any preamble, as if she knew him reasonably well instead of having only glanced at him once.

'No. I was just on my way up to have a shower. I've been sightseeing all day. Then a solitary dinner.'

'I . . . Look, don't hesitate to say no to this. I'm just driving over to a house at Stinson Beach. Jerry said you *might* be willing to go with me. We think there's a chance that David's friend

Fred Wheeler may be there.' She phrased the suggestion with a tentativeness that was at odds with her smouldering eyes full of impatience.

'I'd like to. Give me five minutes?'

'Of course. I must dash out now as I'm triple parked, but I'll just keep on driving round the block till you appear. Must sound an odd invitation, but Jerry seemed to think you're a bit concerned about David. The place I'm driving to belongs to Leonard Troy, near Stinson Beach. Absolutely isolated, standing practically on a cliff edge. Jerry's in Santa Barbara and won't be able to get back till late tonight.'

'Right. Dependent on honourable ancient lift functioning, not more than five minutes.'

'Fine. I'm driving Troy's Tiger.'

Going up in the lift, Buchanan reflected that Cherry Kinsella was both more and less attractive than he had judged from meeting her momentarily in Sally Walters's house. Close to he could see that she had perfect teeth, a finely shaped mouth, and her brown eyes were even larger and more expressive than he had remembered. But these attributes had been somewhat eclipsed by his impression that there was a hard streak in her, something to do with her unusually strong jaw-line and the haughty way she held her head: she conveyed a subdued kind of insolence.

Buchanan's sensations of hunger and tiredness had vanished and been replaced by simple excitement. At one stroke he was back in the game with a chance of finding out more about the David Resznik affair, and the prospect of an evening with a most attractive girl. Cherry Kinsella, despite her momentarily nervous expression when they met, looked capable of surviving most events; he felt less guilty about the idea of stringing her along than he would have done at the prospect of telling lies to Mrs Walters.

After racing along the hotel corridor to his room, he found a blue cardboard box done up with a white ribbon on his bedside table, containing two shirts so well laundered and folded that they looked brand new in their cellophane packets. He mentally thanked American-Chinese efficiency and managed to clean his teeth and shower in under five minutes.

The mirror-lined lift endorsed the opinions Buchanan had been given about 'mish-mashed teeth' and 'cold eyes', but his physical defects did not weigh at all heavily: of one thing he was quite certain – that he was of no personal interest to Miss Kinsella.

The Sunbeam Tiger was parked just outside the hotel. Cherry Kinsella got out as he appeared. She wore a long black sleeveless jacket and trousers and a lilac-coloured blouse. She gave him a slightly more friendly smile, but there was still something critical and defensive about it as if she did not quite approve of him. 'Will you drive? Jerry told me that you'd done some racing. I shall feel embarrassed.'

'Nonsense. Anyway I can't drive here. No licence.'

'Right then.' She got into the driving seat and held the other door open. 'If you won't drive, then eat.' She handed him a paper bag. 'You said something about dinner so I bought you a sandwich. Roast beef in what they call French bread. From David's, a Jewish place in Geary. Very good. But the French bread is a small kind of loaf so it's impossible to eat it and be dignified.'

'Dignified? That's the impression you have of me is it?'

London Western, have been closed for some time, but a lot of dignified and reliable. Concerned about Dave." I think I'm quoting fairly accurately.' She drove off with a surge of power, turning right and right again. 'We go up on to Van Ness and then take the 101 all the way to the Golden Gate Bridge. Have you been across it yet?'

'No. I've only done a little conventional sightseeing in the city. Apart from the trip with Jerry to Hunters Point.'

Cherry ignored his gambit about Hunters Point, but he was not sure whether she did so intentionally or because she had missed it in concentrating on her driving. She drove in what rally-drivers call an 'ear-'oling' style, pressing as hard as you can all the time, taking all bends on the throttle, forcing a way through traffic. She switched on the radio to catch a burst of what sounded like 'The Grateful Dead', turned it up very loud then flicked it off. A perceptible change of personality had set in once she started driving. Her nervousness had been replaced by an aggressive self-confidence. Buchanan could see that her eyes were made up but not her lips. She had some tiny binoculars suspended from a fine gilt chain round her neck, but no jewellery.

'Did you actually race – I mean professionally?' She turned to look directly into his eyes as though to check the truth of his reply.

'Yes. For nearly three years. It's one of those occupations where you get a lot of starters and very few who finish. Just a handful make it. I didn't.'

'Jerry said something about a crash.'

'I had more than one. I had a bad shunt in Germany, at Nurburgring. Broke some ribs and lost a few teeth in that one. Then I had another at Brands Hatch, at Clearways. That's a right-hand bend which kind of falls off on you as you're going round it. Very long and difficult. Lots of drivers have trouble with it.'

'So after that you gave up?' Her assumption was incorrect but Buchanan did not feel inclined to tell her so.

'More or less. Now I just sell cars. Mostly sports jobs like this Tiger.'

'And you enjoy that?' Again there was a hint of faint surprise and condescension in her tone. Buchanan had detected an upper class background for Cherry Kinsella, and there was probably a daddy who was willing to keep sending her cheques so that she could find interesting and exciting things to do, without bothering about tedious matters like earning a living. Now that her nervousness had evaporated Buchanan was convinced that Resznik had not confided in her – she was only in on the edge of his affairs, like Jerry Harland and Leonard Troy.

'Only so-so. It happens to be the one thing I know quite a lot about. Tell me, why do you think Fred Wheeler might be at this place, at Stinson Beach?'

'He went there once before. In May he and David got into some trouble with the police in Berkeley. Over a protest march that ended up violently. Leonard let Fred use it then, as a hideout. And this morning, early, Jerry Harland got a phone-call that he was there. Jerry wanted to see Fred but he had to go to Santa Barbara on an urgent business matter.'

It was plain that Harland had not worried her with the fears that had been induced in him by going to Hunters Point. Cherry still believed that the trouble in which David Resznik and Fred Wheeler had been involved was of the kind so common among militant student radicals, some relatively mild matter which would soon be forgotten or could be handled by a clever lawyer. Buchanan remembered Leonard Troy talking on the phone about 'this very important person. We'll have to do it his way.' Perhaps Troy and Harland had gone off to Santa Barbara to consult him.

They could see the Golden Gate Bridge and it looked even more impressive at night, a great arc of lights miraculously suspended between the dark sea and the sky. Traffic was heavy on the 101 and occasionally got bogged down, but Cherry continued to drive with a total lack of caution, whipping over from one lane to another, using a great surge of acceleration at the lights, constantly challenging all competitors, all part of some internal Grand Prix. When he first got into the car Buchanan had thought that the exhibitionist display had been put on for his benefit, but now he realized that Cherry drove like this habitually. There was an excitement in her eyes that could be catching. He watched her thin wrists and her ankles that showed between the black trousers and the espadrilles as she stabbed on the accelerator or brake. It was plain that she liked danger, and no doubt it was thrilling stuff to be associated with David Resznik operating in the shadows of law and order. But had she any idea of the possible consequences, did she know what bones looked like when they were pushed out from bleeding flesh? He was not going to tell her, but he felt nearly in the mood for handing out a moral tract.

Cherry looked at him with an amused expression. 'By the way, how did you get on with Jerry?'

'All right. He can drink! We made a tour of the clubs last night looking for anyone who might have information about your mutual friend Wheeler. It lasted about five hours and we were drinking most of the time. After a while I had to nurse a beer, but Jerry was still downing Canadian Club.'

'Did he take you to Finnochios?'

'No. Why?'

'I just wondered. Can you understand him all the time? As

89

you've only been out here a couple of days I should have thought some of his conversation might have baffled you.'

'Sometimes, when he was talking with his friends. Like, man, it was really a stoner . . . lay it on . . . !'

'We're into this bad vibes situation,' Cherry suggested.

'Yeah man, it'll curdle your vibes and rigid up your colloid.'

Cherry laughed quite naturally without a trace of nervousness or self-consciousness for the first time since they had met. 'Yes, what does it all mean? No, forget that. I now know it means hardly anything. All that gobbledy-gook, you could boil it all up and nothing would remain. Lots of the young people here are as hooked on words as they are on pot or hash. If you knew the hours I've spent listening to "that's an eros logos principle trip . . . turn on your throat chakra, which is your universal love chakra".'

'But you still like it here? You're going to stay?'

'Not much longer. I want to get back to London. I live on a boat there and I don't like leaving it for months on end. Might get back and find my home had been sunk without a trace. But I can't leave till I know about David.'

Buchanan felt a surge of guilt and other unpleasant feelings as she said this last sentence. When they had stopped on the bridge to pay the toll he had been overwhelmingly conscious of the fact that David Resznik's body had been recovered from the sea at a point more or less beneath them. But he steeled himself about lying to her as he was hopeful that his undercover work would help to find David Resznik's killers as well as stopping their plot.

'I understand that you're friendly with David's grandfather.' Her tone was slightly dubious. 'David always told me that Abe was rather a loner. But you live near him in Wapping? That's right?'

'Friendly is an exaggeration, but I know him quite well. I see him fairly often in the evenings. He goes to a couple of pubs, The Three Suns and the Old Star, that I pop into sometimes. He lives in Reardon Street which is just round the corner from my flat. And occasionally I'll see him in another pub, the China Ship in Orton Street. The China Ship is the only building standing in

Orton Street, all the rest were destroyed by bombs in the last war. That's when Abe's wife was killed. They lived in Orton Street till 1940.' He found it easy to make a smokescreen of factual stuff about Abe Resznik and Wapping with which to bewilder Cherry. She would have to know a lot to catch him out on that ground.

'Wapping is unexplored territory to me. I don't think I've ever been east of Tower Bridge.'

'Its fate is to be just another smart place where trendy people live I'm afraid. As they keep knocking wharves down and opening up the river front there are magnificent sites for flats, and only fifteen minutes walk from the City.'

'And you don't like that idea?'

'Not at all. I like it as it was, and still is to a certain extent, a part of working London. I was born in Hanbury Street, that's near the Whitechapel Road, so I know the East End well. Of course the big docks in Wapping, the St Katharine's and the London Western, have been closed for some time, but a lot of the wharves still operate. There's a big spice-mill and warehouse in Hermitage Wall, and the air round about is often fragrant with spices.'

'David told me that most of the pre-war buildings were knocked flat during the war.'

'Not the wharves along Wapping High Street. There's a combination of the old wharves, the bomb sites and some good new council flats. And the bombed parts have a strange fascination. If you walk along Scandrett Street you would think that St John's Church was rather fine with a handsome old clock on the tower. Turn into Greenbank and you see there's nothing left apart from the front wall.'

'David plans to return to London this winter to see old Abe, so I suppose I shall get to know it too.'

Buchanan opened the paper bag and took out his sandwich and offered it to Cherry. 'Would you like a bit? Plenty for two.'

'No thanks. I cheated by eating mine on the premises.'

The roast beef was excellent and there was slice upon slice of it. Buchanan took a large, undignified bite. He had talked enough about Wapping and he hoped that while he ate the conversation might take a turn away from the tricky subject of Abraham Resznik.

Cherry said: 'Did you see the notice about the Redwood Empire? I shall take the US1 after Sausalito and then we skirt the Muir Woods and Mount Tamalpais for Stinson, but David and I have often driven due north from here, sticking on the 101 right up to the Redwoods State Park or Clam Beach. It's beautiful there – the Redwoods are magnificent and the beaches are superb even though the sea's too cold for swimming. David's very active but now and again he likes to get away.'

'You mean active in politics?'

'He's committed.'

'What does that mean?'

'It means he cares, really cares, about the state the world is in.'

'Don't most people?'

Cherry shrugged. 'They may, but if so they do nothing about it. Fred Wheeler says the test is if you're willing to *try* to change things. Are you a stand-up guy is how he judges people. Well, David is. God, I hope we can contact Fred tonight. I am very grateful to you for coming along. Frankly the house at Stinson, Troy's place, scares me. It's tucked away in a grove of trees with the sea just at the back. Idyllic on a fine day. But not at night, thank you! No one else lives within about a mile. And the atmosphere of the house is strange, full of all this old furniture and stuff from Troy's parents' home in Hollywood. Like a museum of the 1920s.'

Once they had turned off the 101 the traffic diminished till it became quite light. They were travelling through a heavily wooded area with very few houses. It was a pleasant drive to make at night with an attractive girl, but as their headlights picked out a corniche-type road ahead of them Buchanan winced mentally, for Cherry had a habit of losing the tail of the car on tight corners and then over-correcting. As if prompted by telepathy she suddenly asked him: 'What does all that stuff about under-steer and over-steer mean?'

'Under-steer is where you have the car not steering itself round a corner to the same degree as you would expect – it's achieved by braking heavily or an abrupt steering motion. Over-steer is the opposite, where the back wheels are swinging out, controlled skidding really. You may start to go round a corner braking heavily, putting on a lot of lock to set the car up, then you'd let off the brakes and take it round on the throttle.'

'Show me!'

Buchanan shook his head and was silent for a few moments. 'I'm afraid you would be disappointed in my driving, Cherry. I just go from A to B. Nothing at all fancy. You see . . . when we were talking earlier . . . you were wrong in thinking I gave up racing because of my accidents. My parents were both killed when a lorry crashed into their Mini. My father was the kind of man who never drove at more than sixty in his life. One of the tyres on the lorry blew and it just came across the centre section on a motorway – blotted their car out.'

'How terrible! I'm sorry . . . ' Cherry reached out to touch the back of his left hand with her right.

'Yes, it was terrible – for my mother. My father was killed out-right, it would have been a matter of seconds. But my mother lived for sixteen hours.'

It was an act of emotional self-indulgence to talk of the matter that dogged his existence; there was no way of explaining how, for him, the occasion of seeing his mother dying in hospital had been the moment when the partition dividing a sane, reasonable-seeming world from a nightmarish one had momentarily crumbled, or its profound effect on him, but it was some relief just to express the bare facts.

Cherry made a sympathetic noise, a combined sigh and murmur, then said: 'It's funny . . . I didn't think . . , well, that there would be any kind of really intimate conversation with you. I thought you were too buttoned-up. I was wrong.' She turned to give him a genuinely friendly look: an expression which offered a new kind of relationship. As they travelled on there was an intimacy in the silence and Buchanan felt that a bond had been established between them.

13

'This is it.' Cherry swung the car off the road as if she had decided to commit suicide by piling it up in the pine-wood, and they shot through a gap on to a track that had once been concrete but was now going back to a surface of weeds and grass. The moment she had braked she turned her pale face towards Buchanan with an unhappy expression. Suddenly she looked more than just tired; it was as if she had keyed herself up to an effort which had left her exhausted. There was the curious, sedated look about her eyes which he had noticed at Sally Walters's house in Laguna Street.

'The house here is called Olsen's. A man named Olsen built it sometime in the 1930s. Troy called it something else, some word he got out of a book by Herman Melville, but all the local people still call it Olsen's. Frankly, for my money, I know it's quite a beauty spot and all that, Olsen can keep it. It gives me the creeps at night.'

Cherry got out of the car and walked round as Buchanan followed her example, giving him a slight push as he straightened up. 'I say, don't I sound an awful gloom merchant and scare-monger! It's nerves, tension, whatever.'

There was just room to turn the car round at the point where they had been stopped. Olsen's was half-hidden by pine trees but at a distance it looked an attractive house, with white walls and a verandah. The setting was spectacular: where the pine trees thinned, at the left of the house, Buchanan could see the moonlit Pacific. He stared up at the sky which appeared to be made of dark blue velvet sprinkled with silver stars. A breeze stirred the tops of the trees, filling the air with the scents of pine and the sea. He said: 'I certainly shouldn't employ you if I wanted to sell the house.'

Cherry held his arm lightly as they walked towards the verandah steps. 'All right then. It's what they call Spanish Colonial style with wooden columns and a roof of heavily twisted tiles. Inside there's a lot of rather splendid panelling.'

It was the kind of place where an air of former elegance accentuates its current neglect and delapidation. Some of the tiles were broken and a section of the verandah floor had collapsed, while the whole house was under siege by threatening undergrowth which was trying to reclaim the site.

'No lights. On the other hand, all the curtains are pulled. Fred may have been here and just gone off for a while. I'll check on the key. Troy leaves a spare one hidden in that pot.'

Cherry bent down and used both hands to tilt a heavy earthenware jar which stood close to the front door, then reached into it tentatively as if scared of encountering a snake. 'No key.'

Buchanan tried the door. 'On the other hand, you don't need one. This isn't locked. Shall we go in?'

The atmosphere inside the house was musty and damp, as if the contents had been imbued with sea mist and were never properly aired. When Buchanan pushed the door open Cherry reached around him for a light switch. The click turned on two old-fashioned standard lamps which stood in corners of the room and a wooden-bladed fan which began whirring heavily with spasmodic lapses.

The room was large but the crowded furniture had a diminishing effect. Wooden panelling helped to make it dark, along with brown curtains, leather chairs and the dried-leaf colour of the carpet. One wall was practically covered with photographs, and others in gilt and silver frames, along with innumerable knickknacks, stood on small tables and other flat surfaces including the top of a large radiogram cabinet.

Cherry sighed. 'You see what I mean. Nostalgia-ville! As Jerry says, the past is a nice place to visit but I don't want to live there.'

She began opening doors in the passage that led out of the living-room, holding her nose in one place and exclaiming: 'Yikes! It seems that a cat has been shut up there. Claustrophobia, your name is Olsen's. Look, we don't have to sit here. We could go down to the beach for a few minutes so that you can say you've paddled in the Pacific, or something. Meanwhile we can leave all the doors open to air the place. I'll scribble a note for Fred just in case he comes back while we're sliding down the cliff.'

Cherry picked up a pencil and wrote a few words on a note-pad which lay by the telephone and a small table-lamp. 'There, that'll do. Let's escape for a few minutes. When we come back I'll make some coffee. Or we could have a drink. As you can see, there's a bar and it's laden with bottles.'

They made their way along a gloomy passage which was cluttered with large cartons. 'All this is the result of Troy's mania for collecting things and his schizophrenic attitude. He loves this place, he's mad about the sea, a mother image or something like that, wants to be here and, I suspect, secretly plans to come back when he gives up his business. But Jerry doesn't like it and, as you've probably guessed, what Jerry says goes. That's love I suppose. So Troy holds on to it, but the place becomes more and more like a neglected museum.'

The back door opened reluctantly as it had to be forced back against the springy arms of a bush. Cherry found another large earthenware pot to hold it open. The ground sloped down steeply and an ink-coloured sea with white-crested waves could be seen through and beyond the dwindling grove of pine trees. Cherry stood still and silent. It was difficult to know whether she was just contemplating the view or sorting out some internal clue about Olsen's and Fred Wheeler. She said: 'The world seems rather unreal at night. A more dangerous place somehow.'

As they walked towards the sea Cherry took Buchanan's hand. Her hand was thin and cold, very different from Laura Mayhew's which subtly transmitted her sensuous nature. Cherry said quietly: 'Of course, I had been warned that David and Fred were involved in some trouble, that something had gone wrong. Otherwise I'd have been scared stiff when David went off like that. I think he may have gone to L.A., he's got some good friends there. But if the trouble's really bad I can't understand why Fred didn't go with him, instead of hanging around here, surfacing suddenly in the Haight, and so on. And why can't they contact us now?

Why hasn't Fred phoned Jerry? He knows Jerry's a real pal, absolutely dependable.'

Buchanan could not think of anything to say: often there had been occasions in the past when he had longed to express himself with urbane fluency, now he searched for any banal remark that would bridge an extremely difficult situation. He knew where his loyalty lay, but it was difficult to walk hand-in-hand with a girl he now found sympathetic and to keep telling her lies.

Cherry said: 'I'm convinced Fred must have been here. I said Troy is generous with his possessions but that doesn't mean he likes just anyone using Olsen's, or Starbuck, which is what he calls it.'

'Starbuck? That's the name he uses as a cable address for his business. Starbuck, San Francisco – I spotted it on his writing-paper in the window at Ocean-Exotica.'

'Yes? Well, it's a name out of Melville, you know, the chap who wrote *Moby Dick*. Troy called the house Starbuck too. It just came back to me.'

They had reached the cliff edge. Below them there was a cove with a small headland on the left-hand side and a much larger one on the right. Even by moonlight Buchanan could see that the sand was a darkish colour. Steep steps had been cut in the cliff and these were secured by pieces of wood. Cherry led the way, still holding Buchanan's hand. She said: 'I hope your first sight of the open Pacific isn't too much of a disappointment! Of course, I've been spoiled. I was brought up in Connemara and I think we have the world's finest beaches there. White sand backed by grassy cliffs with horses grazing on them, little pools by the rocks. The sea here is so sterile. Beyond that headland on your right you come to Stinson Beach proper. Miles of it, and you can walk the whole length without seeing a single shell or a starfish, anything like that.'

'Do you go back to Ireland? Does your family still live in Connemara?'

'No. My dad lives in Dublin, and my mama went off with an Englishman, some horrible stinking rich guy. The last address I had for her was Portofino. Ah well! Shall we run down the last bit?'

Without waiting for a reply she tightened her grip on his hand and started running down a slope parallel with the steps. It was exhilarating to pound down the cliff, attaining a momentum that they could not control. On the beach they had to run in an arc which just kept them out of the breaking surf.

Cherry said breathlessly: 'That was good. And I needed it, much more than a drink. I hate the smell in Olsen's, makes me think of death somehow.' She let go of Buchanan's hand and stared out at the moonlit sea full of glittering movement and eyed shadows. 'Just at this moment I feel a little demented. What with this place and worrying about David. I mean, if nothing happens, if Fred doesn't turn up, what can I do? Sally wants to contact the police and I have to diplomatically ward her off by pretending there's nothing really to worry about. Yet she must know that I know . . . Look, I'm sorry to burden you with all this. I keep forgetting your interest in these goings-on must be slim. I could be developing into a great bore from your point of view.'

'Nothing about this evening has been boring. Far from it. I just wish I could help.'

'You *have* helped simply by coming here. I couldn't have faced it alone and yet I'd have hated missing any chance.' She glanced down at her tiny wrist-watch. 'We'll make our way back. It's 9.30. The house will have had a blow through by now and I could use some coffee.'

Buchanan bent down and bathed his hands in the sea. It was much colder than he had expected. He splashed some water on his face, saying, 'Freshening-up ritual pre entry of Olsen's. Frankly I found the atmosphere there rather depressing myself.'

As they walked back across the beach Cherry took his hand again. It was an unusual experience for Buchanan to hold a girl's hand without getting any sexual reaction at all: with her it was just a sign of friendship. He was puzzled at how much his impression of her had changed in the course of a few hours. She seemed to be an entirely different person from the rather hard, haughty looking girl in the foyer of the Hotel Jerome. But it was undoubtedly a mutual matter: they both assumed masks in public.

Climbing the cliff steps, he said: 'Have you tried phoning David's friends in Los Angeles?'

Cherry seemed to pick her words with care. 'They are all pre my era and I don't know their names. David got to know them a couple of years ago when he lectured in L.A. He goes there fairly often still, but I've never seen the place apart from passing through the airport.'

The breeze had freshened in the time they had been on the beach and there was a continuous motion in the pine trees. An owl screeched. Cherry looked round when they glimpsed the house and said: 'Talk about a lonesome place.'

Buchanan knew nothing of fine wines or *objets d'art* but he considered himself a connoisseur of loneliness; travelling round the Mediterranean he had accumulated considerable experience of lonely evenings, deserted sea fronts, radios blaring in empty cafés, despairing drunken voices calling out in the night. He found the accumulation of junk in Olsen's depressing, but not the siting of the house. If it was cleared and properly opened to the air he could enjoy living with the right woman in that isolated situation. He was coming more and more to envy happily married couples and to fancy the prospect of settling down.

Cherry said: 'Oh dear! The house looks exactly as we left it. So, no Fred I'm afraid. You won't mind if we hang on for a bit? Do you like music? Troy's got a vast horde of discs, mostly golden oldies.'

'I'm a reggae fan, West Indian music. And early Beatles like "From Me to You", "Baby Let's Play House".'

'Nothing like that on these premises I'm afraid.' Cherry hesitated for a moment at the back door and took a deep breath. 'Here we go. You wander through to the living-room and I'll make some coffee.'

'Right. I think I *may* open one of Troy's bottles, as he's rich and generous.'

'Ah yes, I should enjoy that now.'

The living-room was much less musty and Buchanan closed the front door. He walked behind the bar and picked up a bottle of Remy Martin brandy and two glasses, then set them down on the table by the phone. The room looked more like a second-hand shop than somewhere to live, crammed with invention and redolent of a past era. From the wall of photographs scores of faces seemed to clamour for attention. Girls with bee-stung lips, pencilled eyebrows and bobbed hair stared at him with knowing smiles, heroes with square jaws and lots of greased black hair held intense expressions. They said – we too were young, we fell in love, for a while we took the centre of the stage. It was a salutary record of the fleetingness of time.

Buchanan turned away from the world of shadows and poured himself an inch of brandy before idly picking up the note-pad on which Cherry had scribbled some words to Fred. He was interested to see her writing which was small and neat, with sharply pointed letters that hinted of nervous energy.

Beneath the pad there was a loose page which had been torn from it. Elaborate doodling that chronicled the journey of a pin-headed man filled the top half, but beneath the drawings there were some phone numbers and jottings which he recognized as being in David Resznik's hand:

> Enterprise Constructions
> Quicksilver?
> Starbuck, San Francisco
> Quicksilver, San Francisco?
> Quicksilver, New York?
> J. L. Garve?

Enterprise Constructions meant nothing to Buchanan, but the word quicksilver hit him with the force of a punch. He could hear Jack Collier saying that it might hold the key to the mystery surrounding Resznik, that David had been puzzling over it himself, and that a page of his diary contained the dictionary definition. Here was further evidence of his obsession with the word, and an indication that he had reached the theory of it being someone's cable address. The name J. L. Garve was equally interesting, but in a tantalizing fashion as he remembered seeing it somewhere but could not place the connection immediately. As he brooded on this he heard the sound of cups rattling and pocketed the piece of paper before Cherry appeared in the doorway. She had combed her hair and looked fairly relaxed, pulling a funny face.

'You'll be amazed to learn that I've calmed down now – feel nearly normal. Oh well, one can't go on worrying all the time. *Che sarà sarà.* Just at the moment I feel like relaxing a little. The coffee is hot and strong. And I'd like some of that cognac too, please.'

Cherry put the tray down and looked around the room. 'I must say we improve this place enormously. It seems nearly like a home.' She walked over to the large, old-fashioned radiogram. Records were kept in a cabinet, in large stainless-steel racks, and in precarious piles by the wall. When she opened the lid she turned to look at Buchanan with an apprehensive expression. Buchanan heard the sound of a branch being snapped outside. Cherry held a record up and said: 'It looks as if David has been here recently! This – *Fidelio* – was on the turntable. It's a great favourite of his and he always played it when he came here.'

Buchanan heard another noise outside the house. He stood up and said: 'I think someone's prowling around out there. I'll go and see. Don't worry. Just put a record on and wait here.'

Excitement made him oblivious of the gloomy passageway and kitchen. In a moment he might confront the elusive Mr Fred Wheeler. He turned off the light in the kitchen, paused and then stepped outside. Holding his breath, keeping quite still, he was sure he could hear someone moving about in the undergrowth at the side of the house. He walked along by the back wall and then braced himself with his hand, which touched some window-invading plant, to look round the corner.

Five or six yards away a stocky Negro faced him. The Negro held an unusually large pistol in his left hand, gripping it by the long barrel. He said in a slurred voice: 'Stop, man, or I'll blow you up.'

Buchanan did not react well to threats in any circumstances and this was a heads-I-win-tails-you-lose situation. He remembered Collier's description of Resznik's head being smashed in like an egg. At that moment the threat about shooting was a bluff, as the clumsy revolver had to be turned round. Buchanan knew he could move a long way in a few seconds. He raced across the intervening ground and kicked the Negro in his left knee-cap as they collided. When he worked in France Buchanan had been kicked both in the knee and the crotch. He would have been hard put to it to say which he'd enjoyed least. The pain of both was exquisite.

The Negro was swinging the hand-gun round as the kick connected, and his blow caught Buchanan glancingly on the side. The next moment the two of them were bowled head-over-heels together by Buchanan's momentum. It was quite a spectacular display of acrobatics which would have been difficult to repeat. The Negro let out a long grunting growl of pain. They rolled over and over down the hard sandy slope, hands scrabbling on it in vain. Buchanan felt as though all the breath had been knocked out of him, but he clawed at the ground like an animal determined to be the first to get up on his feet. The race for that position was all important. The Negro was strong and game, like a wounded bull, but his left leg crumpled beneath him as he tried to stand. Buchanan stamped on his left wrist and then hit him with two punches that carried every ounce of his weight behind them.

The Negro's face was distorted with pain but he managed to get up on his right knee and swing the long-barrelled Colt against Buchanan's thigh. Buchanan winced, then leant forward and down to hit the Toulouse-Lautrec figure with a rocking right-hand jab. His fist travelled only ten inches but it was a pole-axing blow, and the coloured man took it on the point of his chin. His eyes flickered then closed, and his jaw hung slack. As he toppled forward Buchanan delivered a murderous rabbit punch. Until he could prise the revolver from those big black fingers Buchanan knew he stood a good chance of ending up dead.

The stocky figure slithered indifferently further down the slope with his arms twisted beneath him. Buchanan hurried to turn the unconscious body over, picked up the Colt gingerly and unloaded it, throwing the bullets towards the cliff edge. He said: 'It was a pleasure to do business with you.' His heart was racing wildly, blood dripped from a cut on his forehead, he was bathed in sweat, and now the excitement was over he could feel the pain from the pistol-whipping blows he'd taken on his ribs and thigh. He went through the Negro's pockets, finding only a packet of cigarettes and a gold lighter. The coloured man wore a gold chain round his bull-like neck, and on his wrists a gold watch and a gold identity bracelet. The name S. P. Dinsdale was engraved on an oblong disc. Buchanan pocketed the bracelet and walked up the slope, holding the Colt by the tip of the barrel. He wanted to find a place to hide the pistol so that it could be recovered later, intact with Dinsdale's prints, by the San Francisco police, but he did not know how much time he would have before the Negro came round.

Buchanan leant against a wall of the house getting back his breath, and slipped the Colt into the large pot which stood by the front door. As he did so a crashing sound came from the front of the house, followed by a subdued impassioned murmur and a scream. The scream had a savage, raw, quality – the kind of noise which has to be torn from a human body. He ran through the passageway oblivious of the pain in his leg, drawn by the scream like a magnet.

Bursting through into the living-room, throwing back the door so that it rocked on its hinges, Buchanan found a chaos that resembled the creation of a demented mind. All the photographs on the panelled wall and practically every other small movable object in the room lay smashed on the floor with scores of broken records. The telephone had been torn from its connection at the wall. Tables were overturned and only one lamp was still intact. Cherry lay full length on the floor, an arm twisted behind her back, sobbing. A slightly-built man of medium height, with black hair and sallow complexion, faced Buchanan. He looked relaxed and amused. In one hand he held an iron bar and in the other a vase which he flung at Buchanan's head as he retreated to the door, following it with a stream of other objects. The accuracy of his throwing was that of a professional juggler. He stood in the open doorway for a moment, saying tauntingly, 'Come on, come on,' then sprang outside.

Buchanan followed him, ducking immediately afterwards as the iron bar flashed towards him. It did not hit him but took him off balance, and he fell. Lying spread-eagled, he was conscious of mocking laughter in the dark and then a hoarse voice calling out: *'Fous-moi le camp, gros cochon! Espèce de con! Ça t'apprendra peut-être . . .'*

Getting to his feet seemed a difficult job: there was a hissing noise in his ears like jet engines starting up, and Buchanan felt that complicated messages had to be sent to mutinous parts of his body. He was not sure exactly how much time elapsed between his fall and struggling to his feet. He could hear shouting voices on the otherwise silent road. When he ran to the end of the concrete track he saw a dark-coloured Dodge Challenger being turned around about fifty feet away. One of the doors was open and the Negro was struggling to get in while the car was in motion. A moment later the Challenger swirled off in the direction of Sausalito.

Cherry was standing at the front door. Her face was white and tear-stained. 'Thank God it's you! Like a madman but he wasn't mad . . . Twisted my arm till I thought it would break . . . Then smashed everything up in front of me . . . Kept smiling all the time . . . '

'But who is he? And the other one? There was a Negro outside. I had a fight with him, we slid down the slope and I didn't hear what was going on in the house.'

'I don't know about the Negro. The man who smashed up the room is called Jaeckel. Only seen him once . . . And that was across the street . . . Never spoken to him before . . . ' Cherry's sentences continued to pile up on each other in a broken fashion. She shivered and tears ran down her cheeks in inky rivulets. Buchanan said nothing, but led her into the house and sat her down in an armchair. He persuaded her to drink some brandy, then went out to re-heat the coffee.

After Cherry had sipped some coffee he asked her: 'This man Jaeckel – when was it you met him?'

'At a bar – we were at The Garden of Eden, on Broadway, North Beach – the Sunday evening before David went away. We were having a drink there with Fred, and suddenly David got up and said, "There's someone Fred and I have to talk to." Jaeckel was crossing the road from New Joe's as though he was coming to speak to them, but David and Fred hurried out and headed him off. They talked outside, in the street. I couldn't hear what was said but I could see that David was arguing, excited. And that was unlike David, he always keeps his cool. The man Jaeckel looked impassive though, with his hands in his pockets, shrugging. Then he turned and walked away, calling out something over his shoulder. When David came back I asked him who the man was and he said, "Oh that's Jaeckel, a French friend of Fred's" in kind of a bitter voice. But they didn't say anything else. I asked David about it later, when we were alone, but he wouldn't talk about it. I could see he was very worried about something though.'

'But what did Jaeckel want this evening? Why should he hurt you and smash the place up?'

'He said he wanted to know where Fred was. I said I didn't know . . . Said I wanted to find him myself . . . Told him I was frantic because David had gone off too. Then Jaeckel began to laugh. That was the most sinister thing. Just laughing like that. He terrified me.' Cherry shivered and Buchanan crouched down to put his arm round her shoulders.

14

Buchanan insisted on driving back to San Francisco, brushing aside Cherry's objection about his not having a licence. She did not argue the matter, appearing glad to sink back into the seat by his side and stare thoughtfully out of the side window. The coffee and brandy had helped to calm her but she was obviously still upset, very pale and quiet, as though she had withdrawn from her present surroundings to ponder the twist in the situation brought about by the encounter with the mysterious Monsieur Jaeckel. Buchanan was convinced that Jaeckel and Dinsdale were the 'two mean, bad guys' who had been seen with David Resznik at Hunters Point, but he was puzzled as to why two such obvious criminals should have become involved in Resznik's political affairs. Dinsdale looked a run-of-the-mill thug though Jaeckel was clearly something more than that, a very odd type with some sort of bad magic about him. In his dark suit and tie, with his glittering eyes as black as his hair, thin mouth twisted in hostile levity, he appeared like an emissary of Death.

Glancing down at Cherry's slender wrist marked by a bruise, Buchanan wished he was going to have the pleasure of personally feeling Jaeckel's collar; towards S. P. Dinsdale his feelings were more detached, and he reckoned it should not be too long before the San Francisco police had them both safely tucked away.

Cherry had fallen asleep and her face lost its tendency to hardness in repose. She had scrubbed her face clean of make-up after the bout of inky tears, and her closed eyes looked like those of a child, the skin quite devoid of lines. Her poise and sophistication had somehow combined to make him think she might be his contemporary: looking at her as she slept he judged her to be six or eight years younger.

Buchanan enjoyed driving along the deserted road cut through woodland, and he took the corniche section where it followed a series of ravines at a fair speed. The moon was obscured by cloud and in the dark it was a test of driving skill of a kind he had not encountered for a few years. Some of the bends were tight and there was one uphill corner curving left, with a blind apex and exit, like the South Bank bend at Brands Hatch. His main asset as a racing driver had probably been his ability to see everything in slow motion, as it were, so that he was presented with a series of close-ups in fine detail of coming hazards. The surest sign for him of being off-form was simply an awareness of speed: if he knew he was going fast then he was out of touch, as he had known when he hit the Masta Kink section on the Spa circuit in 1966. To be feeling one hundred per cent was essential with a Formula One car, which was like a thoroughbred horse in its sensitivity and nervousness: in a corner it was right on tiptoes, on the very edge of adhesion, so that it had to be coaxed into the apex. With the Tiger there was no need for such gentle handling, but even so taking a succession of tight corners was like bringing a woman to a climax, so that as you started to enter the area of excitement you set up a pace which was right for the car and then guided it through at a rhythm.

Once he had left the corniche Buchanan glanced again at the sleeping girl. He found it an unusual experience to be so close to someone as attractive as Cherry without any stray impulse of sexual desire. Curling tendrils of dark red hair framed her pale face to a heart shape – he could admire its loveliness, her sensitive mouth and the slight curve of her breasts against the lilac blouse, in a strangely objective fashion.

He tried to analyse his feelings about her, judging his sense of guilt in keeping back the fact of Resznik's murder from her; but his thoughts strayed to frankly lascivious memories of Laura, of waking at night to see her breasts rising and falling with the rhythm of her breathing, holding them through the thin fabric of her nightdress so that her nipples became taut and she writhed with sensual pleasure while still asleep. Speeding through the night on an empty country road in Marin County, Northern California, it was odd to think that within two or three days he would be whisked back to London and faced again with the dilemma of his association with Laura. A simple accident had disclosed to him the truth about Laura's husband: tidying some cushions on a couch in her flat after a bout of love-making he had found a letter which had been thrust underneath them. Seeing the words 'All my love' had been enough to make him read on. It had been like learning of David Resznik's death in three words from Jack Collier.

'You may just drive from A to B, Ed, but there is a certain professional smoothness about the ride. I had a nice little nod-off then. Very refreshing.' Cherry smiled as she spoke, but her eyes remained thoughtful.

'Next stop Laguna Street, and I'll deliver you into the excellent care of Mrs Walters.'

'I think you rather fancy Sally. I'm not surprised if you do. But I'm afraid, alas, that I don't want to go straight back to Laguna Street. I want to make another call tonight, but of course you don't have to come. I can drop you at the Jerome.'

'You do realize it's 11.45? Can't you leave it till tomorrow, this call I mean? The world isn't going to run away you know. I prescribe a good night's sleep.'

'A good prescription, no doubt. But I must go there. It's a lawyer whom David consulted a couple of times. I feel I could do with some of his sage advice right now. And it won't be too late for him. I happen to know there's a party at his house tonight. Jerry said he would probably head there when he got back from Santa Barbara. Oh dear! I've lost my binoculars. That horrible man Jaeckel tore them off and threw them somewhere in the room. I forgot all about them till now.'

'Do you want to go back? I can turn the car round.'

'I wouldn't think of it. What's a pair of toy binoculars compared with all of poor old Troy's stuff? I must see Jerry and tell him about the mess at Olsen's. And this lawyer, Charles King, I'll have . . . Oh God, what a mess! I really don't know which way to turn.'

'Your friend Fred Wheeler has a lot to answer for. It's a dangerous game he seems to be playing.'

'Not a game.' Cherry was plainly nettled. 'Anything but that. Fred and Dave have been trying to organize radical opinion here

– channel it so that it can be really felt. When that puts you into direct opposition with the government, and they fight back through tough cops, obviously it's difficult and can be dangerous.'

'Well, I'm a stranger here and don't know much about the set-up, but I'm prepared to bet those two men at Olsen's were just plain thugs. How come Fred gets mixed up with criminal types like that? You didn't see the Negro in the garden, but he's the kind of professional frightener they use in protection rackets.'

'Creepy people like that – oddballs, as Fred would call them – they hang around the fringes of lots of movements. David doesn't approve of them any more than you or I, but it's hard to control everything – sometimes you get allies you regret, you know. This man I want to see – Charles King – he's a lawyer, a very distinguished one, who's helped us – he sympathizes with the radical movement. I suppose the opposition papers would say he belongs to the radical chic. Well, he's wealthy and successful, an important man in his field, but he doesn't like the way things are going in this country so he tries to protect people like David and Fred. He's at one edge of the movement. At the other edge you might occasionally bump into riff-raff like that Negro and Jaeckel.'

Cherry was speaking more frankly now and Buchanan digested this information in silence. He had had his fill of the radical chic during his long tramp round the Haight-Ashbury and North Beach areas. Most of them were like actors, with their Army Surplus poor boy outfits and their let's-get-tough jungle warfare green combat boots with 24-hook yellow lacing. Middle-class élitists playing in the gutter and thumbing their noses at ordinary working men, telling them that their newly won affluence, their possessions and ambitions were nothing but delusions. Buchanan could admire someone like Abe Resznik with a lifetime of hard graft, danger and struggle behind his opinions, but spoilt college boy radicals cashing cheques from wealthy parents they purported to despise were objects of his silent derision. The prospect of going to a party where they abounded in their fake guerrilla gear, screaming their baby orders, come fairly low on his list of pleasurable occasions; but it might mean another lead, and an hour or two's delay in phoning Collier about Dinsdale and Jaeckel could not make a vital difference. He tried the mildest of answers, though hunched in mental opposition. 'I suppose so. There are plenty of freaks about. More of them every day it seems.'

'I thought you must have bumped up against some in your time. You made so little fuss about that fight you had at Olsen's.'

'No superman, me! My ribs still ache. But getting knocked down, that kind of thing, a good deal of the agony is anticipation you see. When it happens, when you actually hit the deck, you find it's nothing much after all. A little bruising, one or two scrapes, so what? And I suppose it does you some good to let off steam. Anything that's been bottled up comes out then. Bumming around the Mediterranean for a couple of years taught me a lot like that. I achieved nothing positive, but experience-wise it was invaluable. For one thing I'm an expert on failure.'

'Sounds a rather negative expertise.'

'Maybe. But useful. I got so used to small businesses that were teetering to disaster, I could see it coming before the people who were running them. Often you have to work harder at a business that sounds like money for old rope than you do at something more conventional. And now I realize how much you've got to want success in order to succeed. Also that you can have a strong aura of success but be doomed to fail.'

'You're never tempted to return to driving – racing?'

'No. I want to find something more worthwhile.'

'Selling sports cars?' Cherry's tone was at once incredulous and faintly amused: there was a hint of the upstage character she had seemed at the Hotel Jerome.

'No – but it's not easy to make a change – my talents and knowledge are limited. I just hope I can sometime, that's all.'

Buchanan could see the glow of lights on the Golden Gate Bridge. 'Where are we heading? I mean, where does this Mr King live?'

'I think I ought to drive again now I feel okay. I should hate the idea of you committing some tiny traffic error and getting dragged off by the cops. Charles King lives at Point Lobos, by Sutro Heights Park. A rather grand house overlooking the Pacific.'

'Somehow – strange to say – I've gone off houses with dramatic views of the Pacific.'

'I promise you that Point Lobos is a very different matter. An elegant, comfortable house with super efficient Chinese servants. Antique furniture, beautiful paintings, and so on.' Cherry said this in an abstracted way, as if thinking of other matters. She seemed to be oblivious of the paradox in the situation she outlined: the ultra-luxurious residence and servants of a member of the radical chic who helped revolutionaries. When Buchanan pulled the car into the side of the road to swop seats a shadow passed across her face, and she said doubtfully: 'Jaeckel? Is that a French name?'

'I don't know about the name but he swore at me in French. I've worked in France and the swearing was authentic. A strange character. He threw things like a juggler and moved – sprang about – like an acrobat.'

'I've never met anyone remotely like him. I felt he was quite ruthless. Would do anything to get what he wanted, but not in a fit of anger. Those dark eyes smiling when he hurt me. I shall dream about him I think.'

15

They drove past a serpentine white wall and what seemed an unending line of parked cars. A massive wooden gate in the wall, with carved panels and decorated wrought iron hinges, was mutely eloquent of grandeur beyond. When Cherry managed to park the Tiger between a Mustang Mach I and a Chevrolet Stingray her breathing was shallow and she fiddled nervously with the ignition key for a few moments as if undecided what to do next. As she got out of the car she gestured vaguely with her left arm. 'Point Lobos. And over there Sutro Heights Park. Adolph Sutro built a mansion here in the 1880s. A penniless German immigrant, he made a fortune on the Nevada Comstock Lode and became a philanthropic Mayor. Now a public park with disintegrating statues, a forlorn-looking gazebo decorated with graffiti like "Toujours, Pooper" and rather beat-up cypresses.'

She looked at the sky where small clouds like grey smoke were scudding across the moon, and said enigmatically: 'Hopes, like sparks, fly upwards,' then pointed towards the low seaward horizon, outlined with silver in the moonlight. 'And there we have what the original inhabitants of this area, the Costanoan Indians, called the Sundown Sea.' She talked continuously, as though she couldn't stop, in a slightly breathless way. 'Out there the Seal Rocks. When you turn left down at Cliff House you come on to the Great Highway running straight for miles and fronting a rather dreary stretch of the Pacific and sand-dunes. But this area, just around here, is interesting. Seriously, you ought to explore it if you can spare the time. Traditionally you begin a walk here by rubbing the belly of the Japanese Temple Guard at 1090 Point Lobos Avenue. He stands beside the totem-pole just north of the restaurant. That's for luck, I was told.' She pulled a wry face. 'I feel like nipping down there now. Jesus, I could do with some luck!'

Buchanan did not feel inclined to say anything else false in an attempt to cheer her up. Very soon she would have to face the fact of David Resznik's death. When he pushed open the heavy gate they saw there were only two cars parked in the spacious drive, a white Cadillac that faced them and a Rolls Corniche turned the other way as if in the hope of avoiding ostentation. A hollow-eyed statue of a man in a Roman robe stared at them across a lawn.

Cherry said: 'A house of Mediterranean inspiration. Designed, I believe, by Appleton and Wolfard. As you may have guessed, Ed, you can add me to your list of failures. I was a student of architecture for two years, dropped that and did a course of Political Science at the L.S.E. Dropped out of that to stay on here with David. And so it will go on I suppose.'

'Rubbish. You're not authentic failure material, and I speak as an expert. Look, if you don't mind I'll wait out here for you. With a plaster over one eye, tears in my shirt and dusty trousers I don't feel quite right for this party.'

'Come on! You're talking nonsense now. No one here will care about such things. Matter of fact, you look rather fashionable – radical chic-wise. The poor man's Ché Guevara! Anyway, we won't stay long. I only want to have a few words with Charles King and then we'll just see if Troy and Jerry are here. I shall need your moral support when I have to tell Troy about that mess at Olsen's.'

They went up shallow, oval steps. The front door was a massive affair like the one in the stone wall, elaborately carved. A moment after the chimes were heard it swung back, opened by a handsome Chinese youth dressed in light grey trousers and a royal-blue cotton jacket that buttoned to the neck. The décor of the hall was white; it was large, and devoid of all decoration apart from one oil painting. From above there came the continuous noise of conversation and the fainter one of music. Cherry smiled at the Chinese servant and then spotted someone half-way up the elegant curving staircase. She said: 'Good. My luck's in for once. That's Charles now. Won't be a sec, Ed,' and hurried over to speak to the man in the dark grey suit who met her at the bottom of the stairs.

The Chinese youth went silently behind a curved glass wall and then vanished from sight like a ghost. Buchanan moved towards the picture. It was an unfinished study of a clown in an old-fashioned white suit and large ruffed collar, with a light brown hat that framed his head like a halo, standing by a donkey. As he walked towards it Buchanan caught a startled glance in his direction from the man with Cherry. There was just a flash of the whites of his eyes, but this momentary impression was strong enough to puzzle Buchanan. He felt quite certain that something about himself had disturbed the sophisticated looking man in the dark grey suit. He pondered this while pretending to study the painting.

'Hi there, Ed! Charles King. You're very welcome.' The man standing by Cherry called this out in a deep, patently masculine voice, not unlike Leonard Troy's, practically devoid of an accent. King flashed a grin and held out a small, well-manicured hand that slipped away as Buchanan tried to shake it. Close to he looked like someone very sick skilfully made up to give the superficial impression of a healthy complexion. 'Come on up now. The party's just beginning to be fun.'

King turned away as Buchanan thanked him and became intent in conversation with Cherry, so that Buchanan followed them up the shallow stairs feeling faintly ill at ease and superfluous.

As they moved along a white corridor decorated with old paintings of clowns, Buchanan recognized the music which was being played with a strong beat. It was The Who's song 'My Generation', and he caught the key line 'Hope I die before I get old'.

The party just overflowed into the corridor, and King introduced Buchanan to a man in a white cowboy suit and a white shirt decorated with dark blue stars who was standing by the open door. 'Ed – Billy. Billy, you get Ed here a drink and break out a dish of those good canapes. Ed, you make yourself at home now, have a drink. I hear you missed out on dinner – Billy will fetch you something. Cherry wants a word or two somewhere quiet.

We'll be five minutes.' He said all this in a quiet, rather lifeless voice, with the authority of someone who expects others to make an effort to listen and then snap to.

Buchanan said 'Fine, fine,' and a moment later Cherry and King had pushed through the crowd and were out of sight.

'Scotch, Ed?' Billy's cowboy suit looked as if it had been bought that afternoon and just taken out of the box; it had piped edging and bronze buttons; it looked a little tight in the sleeves. He wore atomic-reactor type sunglasses which he removed momentarily to disclose shifty yellow-green eyes. He was of medium height and had, for Buchanan, the distinctive look of a professional boxer. Buchanan had done a fair amount of sparring at a gymnasium over a pub used by professional boxers in the East End of London, and he could pick out their easy confidence coupled with a slight swagger. He said: 'Yes, thanks, I'd like that.'

Billy steered Buchanan a little way into the room so that they were within reaching distance of a small table on which there were trays of drinks. 'I'll have to fight my way clear across the room, pal, for that Scotch so why not try this very good Bourbon meanwhile. And hold tight now! Don't move an inch fella or I'll lose you.'

Buchanan took a sip of the excellent whisky and looked around as Billy pushed his way through the centre of the crowd. It appeared as if the party had been going some time for everyone seemed to be well tanked up. The party was an all male affair, boisterous and extremely noisy. A few of the radical chic had declared themselves by camping it up in Army Surplus gear and tramps' clothes, but there were a fair number of dark suits and trendy ranch outfits. Social gatherings without any women Buchanan found boring; he steered clear of stag parties but in his limited experience there was usually the undertone of frustrated queer sexuality about them. He picked up a large biscuit covered with cheese and crab chunks, and listened to the conversation.

'Took off his hair-piece and it was instant Dorian Gray.'

'You come on like a Chief Justice.'

'Okay, Mick Jagger I'm not.'

'But I recognized her immediately, even with her clothes on.'

'Out of sight!'

'I'll draw a veil over what followed.'

'Well as we all know dope will get you through times of no money better'n money will get you through times of no dope.'

'Look, I don't want to crimp things.'

'It's a cop-out from responsibility.'

'Sorry, Ed.' Buchanan turned to find that Billy had materialized at his shoulder. 'I'm told the goddamned Scotch lies thataway.' He pointed towards an open door half-way round the big room. 'Push hard in that direction, fella. I just gotta see you get the right stuff, pal.'

As Buchanan edged his way round the room he was aware of a ripple of excitement in the crowd, as if there had been some kind of announcement which was being passed on from one small group to another. Among the snatches of conversation he thought he heard references to 'Dave' and tried to listen more intently.

'Dave – did they give him a hard time?'

'He's in big trouble.'

'Dave – did he fink on us?'

The repetition of the name Dave and the sudden stir set off a warning-system somewhere inside himself, so that his feeling of tiredness dropped away. They reached the door and he found it led into a much smaller room where it appeared that a party within a party was being held, for there were no dark suits among the men there and they were all very young. Conversation in the small room was particularly excitable and consisted of fragmented sentences punctuated with 'Dave' and 'bull' and the staccato command 'Listen!'

Buchanan wanted to listen, and to make some sense out of the snatches he heard, but his attention was claimed momentarily by a man in a pale brown suit who looked very drunk and smelt of whisky. The drunk said confidentially: 'See that old clown?', pointing to the wall by Buchanan's head where there was an old engraving in an elegant gold frame. The engraving showed an ugly, deformed man with a hooked nose and a massive belly kept in place by a belt. He had golden buttons, red and green ribbons and a black mask. 'Tha's Pulcinella fella. In France known as Polichinelle. Hanswurst in Germany. Old Punch y'see? You know what he says fella? May as well laugh at the world since you'll end up dust. Laugh or cry, s'all same, jus' dust. Cucurucu's 'nother name for him, from the shriek of the cock. You know what? He's right fella. Dust, that's all.' The drunk nodded several times and subsided into silence and a fixed expression of depression.

'Ed – pal – finally – after all these years – I want you should meet Hector McDonald.' Billy had taken hold of Buchanan's arm with one hand; in the other he held up an unopened bottle of Glen Mist liqueur whisky. There was an unpleasant undertone to Billy's teasing, and something subtly threatening in his posture. He had pocketed the fancy sunglasses.

'That's kind, thanks.' Buchanan poured some of the whisky into his empty glass and looked up to catch sight of Leonard Troy on the other side of the big room, regarding him with an Oh-my-God expression. He waved the Glen Mist bottle in Troy's direction and called out 'Hi there – Leonard!', but Troy did not reply though his expression became shamefaced and confused before he vanished from sight. Buchanan felt as certain that he was in a tricky spot, and one liable to become dangerous, as if the floor had shifted beneath his feet. He hoped he masked this by handing the bottle back to Billy and saying: 'Try some. Very good indeed. Even better than the Bourbon.'

'Now tha's real kind of you, Ed! Yes, pally, I might just do that.' Billy poured himself a very small shot, drank it, and then stared at Buchanan with a curious expression in which there was barely veiled contempt.

There had been no audible order of 'Shortest on the right, tallest on the left', but gradually Buchanan was being hemmed around by the biggest and toughest looking men in the room. He rubbed his nose as he often did at moments of danger: he was in no doubt that it existed for him though still not palpable. He did his best to appear unaware of the way things were developing and said to Billy: 'Miss Kinsella? Cherry? Do you think she'll be much longer?'

Billy smiled in an unpleasant way, saying, 'No – not long, Ed. Now drink up pal.' This was against a background of half-hearted conversation in which the name 'Dave' and the words 'fuzz' and 'pigs' began to make some sort of pattern. Suddenly there was another convulsive ripple of excitement in the bigger room, accompanied this time by a visible physical movement. Looking across it, Buchanan saw Leonard Troy again; with another man he was half leading, half carrying Cherry who looked terribly pale. Her eyes were half-closed and she appeared drunk or sedated, incapable of walking unaided.

Buchanan exclaimed 'Cherry! Wait!' and tried to move, but found himself restrained by Billy and two of the other men standing by his side. A blind anger was growing inside himself and he was aware that he had to control it: in his situation he needed to be ice-cool. He said: 'I want to see Cherry. She looks ill.'

Billy said quietly: 'Wait here pal.' Other voices now were directed at Buchanan: 'You know what's wrong, pig.' 'Don't syrup out that goddamned schmaltz.' 'Bull, bull, bull.' 'Don't give us that shit.'

Buchanan said equally quietly: 'I don't want to wait here. I want to talk to Cherry.'

Billy stood with his hands on his hips; as Buchanan was being restrained by so many other hands and arms he obviously felt free to be openly menacing: 'And I say screw you fella! Get him back in there.'

Buchanan was pushed and pulled by a dozen pairs of hands to the back of the small room. Someone punched him in the back and a thin youth pushed his chin upwards. Buchanan protested 'What the hell's going on?' but made no attempt to strike out. He knew from experience there was no joy to be had in fighting a dozen men, and while there was the slimmest chance of lying his way out of trouble he was not going to provoke the mob into more violence.

Only one voice queried what was going on: 'Whatthehell! I mean, what's he done?'

'Screw you Jack. Dave's dead and we're all liable to land up in the pokey. He's some kind of fucking pig.'

'Goddamned pigs. Let Billy work him over.'

Buchanan was held so tightly and pressed in by so many heavy, sweating bodies that he knew it would be an act of desperation to attempt to break out of the pinioning arms; it was a move he would like to make, if only for the satisfaction of hitting Billy once, but he knew it would end in a serious beating for himself.

Among the confused voices he could hear a repetition of 'Let him through' and 'Jerry'. Jerry Harland pushed his way through the crowd, his usually pale expressionless face flushed and contorted with emotion or drink. Propping himself up awkwardly with his stick, breathing heavily, he said: 'Got something interesting here for you to read, Ed old pal! First, though, let me tell you that Troy and I made a trip to Santa Barbara today. To see Fred's girl. She brought us up to date with all the news. She told us that Fred's in Mexico. Apparently someone scared the shit out of him. She told us too about Dave being dead. But you must know about that, Ed old buddy. Troy thought you were too mighty keen on helping us. So he sent a cable off yesterday afternoon, to your good friend Abe. Like to read the reply?'

Harland held a crumpled cable form about an inch in front of Buchanan's eyes. It was addressed to STARBUCK, SAN FRANCISCO. CAUTION. BUCHANAN NOT A FRIEND. VERY SUSPICIOUS. TELL DAVID TO PHONE ME AT LATHAM'S FIRST OPPORTUNITY. REPEAT CAUTION RE BUCHANAN. ABE.

Harland began to talk to Billy: 'Fred's girl told us . . . Apparently Fred thinks that Dave had taken out some kind of insurance . . . He was scared something was going to happen to him – a real crazy affair, this mob Fred got Dave tied into. Anyway, according to Fred, Dave had written out a complete record of all they had done. Names, places, dates, everything, all written down and left in some secret place. It's probably fizzing away right now like a bomb with a time-fuse. And this goddamned character's some kind of British cop, you can rely on it.'

'And Dave's really dead?'

'Fred's sure of it. His girl told us that he'd phoned her twice from Mexico, but she doesn't know where Fred is now. Someone scared the hell out of him and he hasn't stopped running yet.'

Harland waved the cable so that it flapped in Buchanan's face. 'So how do you explain it Ed? Abe thinks you're a suspicious character. Troy does too. And now I'm convinced. I think you're real big trouble.'

119

Buchanan shrugged beneath the restraining hands. 'I think you've all gone mad. I didn't say I was a friend of Abe's. I said I knew him. Troy built it up . . .'

'So you know Abe slightly and yet you want to spend your vacation looking for his grandson! Just an oversized boy-scout. You goddamned liar!'

Buchanan said: 'Ask Cherry about this evening. We went out to Olsen's and two . . .'

Harland broke in. 'You're all confused, Ed. We already heard that tale from Cherry. We don't think you killed Dave. We just think you're some kind of crappy undercover cop and that you'd like to see us in jail. Search him!'

Buchanan struck out with his left arm, pulling the thin youth round as though he were a doll, but it was futile: a moment later he went down on his knees under a cascade of punches and kicks. While he was held down in the corner of the small room the thin youth went through his pockets, handing over the slip of paper with Resznik's notes and the gold identity bracelet to Harland. The thin youth said: 'No gun or badge or anything.'

Harland smiled thinly. 'You jerk! Do you think he's going to carry a goddamned letter from Queen Elizabeth!' He held up the piece of paper. 'He's fuzz okay and this is evidence. That's what he wanted it for all right. I bet you didn't say a word about this to Cherry, did you Ed? Come on! Feed us some more lies! I'll tell you all about this guy. He lies well and he's real sly. He fooled me.'

'And he's full of shit, man,' Billy added. 'But the point is, what the hell do we do with him now?'

Harland said thoughtfully: 'He did some boasting about having been a racing driver. Do you think he's the reckless kind of guy who might get loaded on Scotch and then run out of road?'

Billy laughed. 'By God, Jerry, you're the thinking type man. Tha's just the kind of dude he is. First I'm going to wipe this old bottle of Glen Mist clean of my prints, then we'll give him as much as he wants. Take him down the back stairs.'

Buchanan was bundled out of the door at the back of the small room, pushed and held by so many hands that his feet hardly touched the floor. At some point on the stairs the mob stopped at Billy's command and Buchanan's head was held back and his mouth opened. Whisky was poured down his throat till he gagged. Billy said: 'Yessir, he's the quiet type who suddenly takes to drinking and just don't know when to stop.'

'Really wild!'

'Hold him still a moment,' Billy ordered. 'What I say is, if the poor guy really craves liquor that bad he should have some. I mean man, like the rest of the bottle.'

Whisky flooded Buchanan's throat and more of it slopped into his nose and ears. 'Okay. Any more and he'll be sick at his stomach.'

Buchanan slumped and gave up his struggling resistance, and was only dimly aware that the jostling group had reached the ground floor. The touch of cool night air revived him a little but his only desire was to lie down and sleep. He heard a confused babble of voices but could not make sense of cries about 'car', 'Which car?', 'Really stoned', 'Pig'. His legs felt numb and would not walk. His mind seemed to work with great energy to produce piffling effects like registering that the sky was black. He was vaguely aware of his predicament, but in a detached way as if it was happening to somebody else; he wanted to help this other man who was being strongarmed into the car if he could. He was involved and yet a spectator too. It was like sitting in the 'doghouse' watching someone else having a bad shunt, seeing a car spin off the track at a distance.

After his hands had been pressed on to the steering wheel he was pulled out of the car again and put into the back, lying on the floor. Immediately he struggled up on his knees and vomited. As the car began to move, he fought the bout of sickness and the strong desire to lie down in order to get over into the front seat. The car was speeding downwards without lights. Staring through the windscreen was like looking into a distorting mirror and a kaleidoscope at once. It was a nightmarish situation in that he had to beat the force of gravity to move forward at all. Dream-like, too, in that he felt convinced that nothing would happen to him. He was aware that the car was heading for the black sea if he did not manage to spin the wheel, but it was only a dream sea. He had a sudden vertiginous view, knew that it was too late to control the car, and threw himself on the floor in the front, bracing his body flat against it with outstretched arms as though he was being crucified face down.

16

Steep perspectives. Dull pain and a sense of strain in his eyes. The sensation of everything speeding backwards and close-by objects reeling away into the darkness; then of himself being taken up into the dark sky as if on a giant swing.

Confused images. Moving shadows. His aunt, who had lived in his parents' house for a year when he was a child and conducted a guerrilla war of moods, headaches, 'bad nerves' and slammed doors – why should he be sitting in a taxi, holding her nervously damp hand? He could not make sense of the situation and his changed relationship with her. Bright lights – it was like looking into a prism, all reflected angles. Sharp beams of headlights probed the darkness ahead, showing people scurrying about the damp streets, and memories flooded back. He remembered this momentous journey and their destination, and willed it to be different. Shadows. Whispers? No – sobs, as his aunt cried steadily with her face turned away, looking out of the taxi window at the brightly lit shops full of Christmas decorations.

He could remember times as a child when his aunt had appeared to ransack the house for trouble, straining after some unforgivable insult, prickly with pride. Then her fickle affection for his mother seemed false. Now he knew it was sincere, and its strength was conveyed by the unconscious nervous pressure of her fingers.

An image of a face formed, shivered, then fragmented like a reflection in water broken by a blow. It formed again, against his will. His mother's face, as unnaturally white as though she had been made up like a clown. Her eyes were bloodshot and her hair was stuck to her forehead with sweat. She struggled to raise herself with feeble movements, to lift herself away from tubes, splints and the chromium paraphernalia that surrounded the bed.

He knew from her expression that she intended to say something reassuring, but only a gurgle and blood-stained phlegm came from her lips. She touched his hand. Someone else said in an aside: 'So many fractures, poor thing! We just don't know how she survived. Haemorrhage.' Whispers.

'All right fella? Right fella?' A quavering voice doubled and echoed in his ear.

'Hear me boy? Can you hear me?'

The light was too bright to bear at first, like looking into a searchlight, then it dimmed a little and he could see elderly, identical twins against a background of two shimmering suns. Two seagulls flew past a translucent blue sky. The two grey-headed, blurred faces peered down at him.

'Ah, so you can hear. That's good. Good.'

For a moment he had no knowledge apart from what he vaguely saw and heard. No memories, no information apart from the querulous voice and the face of an old man with silver hair and cornflower blue eyes, but he had a strange feeling of tranquillity as though some great problem had been satisfactorily resolved.

'You've been . . . Your car's all smashed up down there. I say your Chevvy's smashed. One door's off and you must have been thrown out of it here. You're a lucky young fella. Drive off a cliff and you end up on this soft grass. I saw the Chevvy on the beach, then I spotted you. How do you feel boy? What are we going to do with you?'

Buchanan lifted his head and looked round. The patch of grass he lay on was directly below a steep grassy slope. To his right the cliff rose dramatically. A car lay on the rocky beach some thirty feet below him. The whispering noises now resolved into the regular sound of surf breaking on the sand.

'If you were a cat I'd say you'd used up plenty lives driving off a cliff like that. Yessir, twenty feet in either direction and you'd have been in real big trouble. But you can forget your Chevvy.'

Buchanan raised himself on his arms and felt the back of his neck and head where it ached. There was no blood. He grinned at the old man. 'I don't care about the Chevvy. I remember what happened now. Couldn't a few minutes ago. Must have banged my head. Concussion. Pain in my head, otherwise I feel okay. No bones broken I think.'

'You're a Britisher son? Do you live here?'

'Yes, I'm British. Don't live here. Just on a short trip, a vacation.'

'Well now listen to me son. I want you to understand this. You smell mighty strong of liquor and there's a broken bottle of Scotch and an empty Jack Daniels in the old Chevvy. Now can you remember? Was there another car involved? I mean, did you crash into another car?'

'No, I'm fairly sure not. Just went off the road.'

'Even so you don't want the cops in on this right now. Not in your condition. I mean the liquor and all.'

'If there's a phone somewhere near I should like you to call them – the cops. They'll handle it. I feel okay but whacked – very weak. Will you phone for me?'

'This is Point Lobos. Cliff House is just up there. A restaurant. Phone there, I know. I'll gladly make a call if you're quite sure that's what you want.'

'Yes, please.'

The old man stood looking down in silence, pulling a large ear and grimacing as he gave the matter thought. Then he shrugged. 'Well, perhaps that's best. Don't rightly know what else we could do and that's a fact. Name's Ericson. Olaf. I'll be as quick as I can but my running days are over.'

'Ed Buchanan.' He reached up to grasp the old man's hand. 'Thanks a lot, pop. I'm most grateful. Take your time – no rush. I'm comfortable here.'

The delightful sensation of tranquillity, such as he had not experienced since he was a child, had not vanished. He watched Olaf Ericson carefully picking his steps on the sandy slope that led down to the beach, and then looked up at the blue sky and a solitary, fleecy cloud which had a freshly laundered look. His mind had always shied away from the memory of his mother dying, effectively blotting out the traumatic bedside scene, but the vivid dream had been a confrontation that in some odd way had purged the bitterness which had remained in him – a futile bitterness, for it was directed against the vast game of chance that was life itself.

'Ed.' Buchanan heard his name and the slow steps below him, and looked down to see Ericson's silky silver hair again. 'Now listen to me boy. Carefully now. I've been thinking. I'm still not sure you understand the position here son. I make this phone call from Cliff House and we're goin' to have cops out here pronto! So they smell that liquor and see the empty Jack Daniels bottle in your Chevvy – fat chance you'll stand! You being a foreigner, well I don't know if that'll make it better or worse but there's going to be trouble. You can bet on it. Now one of my son's friends is a doc. I could give him a call. Chances are he might be willing to come here, check you out. Course it'll cost you but it'll probably save you too if you see what I mean. We could get you cleaned up some. *Then* you report it to the cops. I mean, it's not as if you crashed into another car. You're the only one who got hurt and you've lost that Chevvy. I should say that's enough punishment for drinking'n driving.'

'Thanks again, pop, but I do know what the position is. I'm thinking quite clearly now. There won't be any trouble with the cops, believe me. If you'll make that call everything will be fine. Okay?'

'Right. Just thought I should check again. You may hear the siren up there before you see me, but I'll be back. Rely on it.'

Buchanan propped himself up on his elbows and lay like that for a few minutes, just looking about and breathing in deeply the salt-tasting air. It was as if all his senses had been sharpened by coming so close to death. It was a beautiful world and he was lucky just to be there, to see the varying blues and greens of the Pacific and hear the gulls screaming as they flew over the cliffs. One of the gulls was outlined by the sun as it glided over the remains of a building and a swimming-bath close to the edge of the sea. Slowly he began to put bits of his concentration in the right place like a jig-saw puzzle. Memories of the previous evening at Stinson Beach came back – of Dinsdale standing in the moonlight and calling out 'Stop man or I'll blow you up,' of Jaeckel saying tauntingly 'Come on, come on,' and his mocking grin as he retreated towards the door; Cherry Kinsella's tear-stained face.

Buchanan laboriously moved his arms to feel in his trouser pockets for S. P. Dinsdale's gold identity bracelet and the scrap of paper he had found by the phone at Olsen's, then remembered that they had been taken from him after Jerry Harland produced the cable from Abe Resznik. But he could remember every word on that list, including the name J. L. Garve which he still found tantalizing. Where had he heard it during his two hectic days in San Francisco?'

Garve, Garve – had he in fact heard it or seen it written down somewhere else? As he brooded over it the visual image seemed to be the right one, then he realized his mind was wandering uselessly. The repetition of the name had a mesmeric effect, lulling him towards sleep. Suddenly he remembered his last sight of Cherry as she was helped from the large room in Charles King's house by Leonard Troy, fainting or dazed with shock, presumably on being told of David Resznik's death. Cherry would also have been shown the cable from Abe and no doubt thought that he had behaved treacherously. It was true, but he did not feel any guilt now. To hell with terrorists and all those who helped them! Terrorists were springing up all over the world – madmen who were determined to achieve their own way by violence and death – they only needed to get their hands on a gun or a bomb to be in business. It was like a rampant, contagious disease and the infection was a completely ruthless fanaticism. His job was to make a small contribution towards stopping it. If that sometimes necessitated devious behaviour, why feel guilty about it?

Dinsdale, Jaeckel, Quicksilver, Garve. Buchanan went over the list of names he had to give to Jack Collier. Villains like Dinsdale and Jaeckel were bound to have criminal records, and with a bit of luck the San Francisco Police might know where to look for them. Collier had seemed impressed by the efficiency of Lieutenant Green and the Homicide Department. David Resznik's notion that Quicksilver, in conjunction with a city, might be a cable address could prove to be another useful lead.

Buchanan gingerly felt his painful neck. He was doubtful whether the police would be able to do anything about the events of the previous night at Charles King's mansion; he knew that retribution for what mobs did when they were drunk was seldom forthcoming. There would be no witnesses for the prosecution, that was certain, and the only tangible evidence pointed to Edmund David Buchanan, one-time racing driver, having driven while drunk and incapable. All he could be definite about was the fact that 'Billy', surname unknown, had poured the best part of a bottle of Glen Mist whisky down his throat – he had no idea who had manhandled him into the old Chevrolet. He was content to leave it in the hands of the San Francisco Police. Now that his cover was blown he would be taken off the Resznik case, and he did not mind that either. He felt profoundly weary, as though he could sleep for a week. His head ached and seemed heavy. For a few moments he watched a gull directly above him and then his eyes would not stay open.

17

The devastation of Wapping by German bombers took place during the first raid of the London Blitz. Wapping Basin and the adjoining Western Dock formed the centre of the great dock fire with which the systematic bombing of London began on 7 September 1940. The *Luftwaffe* broke through the air defences in the afternoon and by six o'clock a vast pillar of smoke rose from this area. By night most of the population of London and its suburbs could see an orange glow filling the sky.

The aftermath of this attack is still clearly visible today. Bomb sites abound and there are other odd relics, such as the pub called The China Ship which is the only building left intact in Orton Street. On either side of its brightly painted premises there are windows of shops which were closed forever in 1940 but still contain adverts of goods available then. Along with the devastation brought by the bombs there is the slower, more subtle alteration wrought by economic changes. The large docks have been empty for years, many of the wharves and cranes are silent and the river laps on deserted quays.

There are plans afoot now to construct a vast complex of buildings on the site of the St Katharine Docks, and when that is completed no doubt other developments will follow and the ambience of the whole area will change. The present period is an interim one and there is an atmosphere redolent of past times and misty melancholy. Old men with dockers' crushed hands sit on warm afternoons in the Tench Street and Waterside Gardens, a few ships are anchored in The Pool with an occasional flurry of activity at one of the 'Stairs', and old buildings like the School of St John, decorated with painted wooden figures of boy and girl scholars in alcoves above the twin doors, slowly disintegrate.

Wapping takes a running jump into the heart of dockland just beyond the purlieus of the City, and its austere yellow brick starts near the Tower of London, but it is a little known area rarely visited by tourists. Edmund Buchanan returned to it early in the afternoon of Monday 18 October 1971. He had jumped off a bus near the Royal Mint and walked along Thomas More Street which winds round a stupendous retaining wall that encircles the St Katharine Docks, built by Thomas Telford in 1825. Buchanan felt as though he was coming home. There was a village-like atmosphere about Wapping, that of a closed community cut off from the rest of London by the Thames to the south and the string of docks extending from Tower Bridge to Shadwell New Basin to the north. Strangers were regarded with suspicion and it had taken some time for Buchanan to be accepted, but now he felt as though he had lived there for years.

Buchanan had spent twenty-four hours in hospital in San Francisco, during which time he had been given a thorough medical examination and found free of after-effects from his crash apart from superficial cuts and bruises. Another forty-eight hours had been passed more pleasantly in the luxury of the St Francis Hotel, lazing about in between conferences with Jack Collier and various members of the San Francisco Police Department.

Collier had booked Buchanan a seat on the Sunday lunch-time TWA 707, telling him to take fourteen days leave, to keep out of Abe Resznik's way, and to move from his flat in Wapping as soon as possible. Buchanan was off the Resznik case for good and would be assigned to other duty when he returned from leave. There was no doubt that at some time in the future he would have to return to San Francisco to give evidence. In the meantime the responsibility for finding out exactly what plot David Resznik had been involved in and capturing his murderers was in other hands. Lieutenant Green, of Homicide, had collated all the information Buchanan could give about the younger Resznik's circle of friends and the events at Hunters Point, Stinson Beach and Point Lobos. Buchanan had heard from Collier that Cherry Kinsella had left the house in Laguna Street and taken a flight for London on the day he had been in hospital. Buchanan still felt a keen interest in all the ramifications of the affair, including the extent to which the radical chic who congregated in Charles King's mansion were tied in with it, but there was nothing else that he could do personally to solve the mystery.

Smelling the unmistakable mixture of river water, tar and spices Buchanan felt sorry that his period of living in Wapping was nearly over. He turned out of the High Street to walk through the narrow passageway at the side of the pub called The Town of Ramsgate; the barrier at the end was unlocked and he was able to get down on the centuries-old stone steps known as Wapping Old Stairs and survey the river scene from the Shad Thames area down to Rotherhithe Pier. The sky above was still blue and clear but mist patches on the face of the river were growing minute by minute. The main body of mist lay downstream, shrouding The Pool, and it was swelling visibly. A barge was being manoeuvred close to the Cherry Garden Pier, otherwise there was little activity and the immobile cranes and gantries took on a ghostly aspect looming above the bank of mist. The only sound was an occasional warning fog-horn from the Limehouse Reach direction.

Watching this familiar scene Buchanan felt restless and undecided as to what he should do. Two weeks previously, before he had known about Laura's husband being in a cancer ward, he would have been knocking at her flat door. The sound of the knock would have resounded on the concrete stairway but there would have been a tardy response. Then the door would have been slowly drawn open while she remained hidden. Now he realized why she was so loath to be seen by her neighbours in the flats as she greeted a male friend. Then there would have been long kisses which never tasted of lipstick or toothpaste but of some unusual sweetness that must have come from her desire and longing for affection.

Shouldering his duffle-bag Buchanan turned away from the river without having formulated any plan apart from the negative decision not to call on Laura – he knew that a succession of those kisses would inevitably lead to the bedroom. He had two weeks' holiday, money to spend, but no inclination to go anywhere. There had been a time when he was so keen on travel that the destination was not important, being just one more fix with the going-away drug; but now he realized that those journeys had been a futile attempt to escape from life.

By the time he reached the old house on the corner of Tench Street and Reardon Path, where he had a small flat on the third floor, Buchanan had decided to defer any decision about the future till he had taken a short nap. The return flight from Los Angeles had been very bumpy as they had flown round a storm and it had been impossible to sleep. He felt that possibly his unsatisfactory mood derived from a combination of feeling tired and the time-lag.

As he opened the front door he heard his landlady, Kate Johnson, upstairs singing 'Red sails in the sunset way out on the blue . . . ' There was a pause, and then the same line was repeated. Mrs Johnson, a sprightly widow, had a vast repertoire of the first lines of popular songs; second lines were always hummed or had to be improvised. She must have heard him, for she appeared in a moment on the stairs, calling out: 'Eddy? Oh, it is you then. Oooh you give me quite a start! You're back quick. Blimey, whatever you done to your poor face?'

'Just a bit bruised, Kate. I was in a car that crashed in San Francisco. Nothing serious. Nobody else was hurt and I only got a couple of cuts and these bruises.'

'Poor you! Aren't you the unlucky one! Fancy going all that way and then having a smash up! Diabolical! I hope you weren't driving and it's going to mean trouble later.' Kate Johnson had been given a garbled version of Buchanan's motor racing career by her grandson, and appeared to regard his driving ability with a mixture of awe and disapproval.

'No, I wasn't driving, Kate. So no trouble. But it was an exciting trip.'

'Did you enjoy it as much as you thought you would? Any chance you might get a job there d'you think?' She thought, as did Laura Mayhew, that he had a rather unsatisfactory part-time job demonstrating cars for a firm owned by one of his old racing friends.

'I wouldn't want to live in San Francisco but I'm glad to have seen it. It's a fantastic city – contains a bit of everything. I bought you a rather nice cup and saucer in Chinatown. You would like

132

Chinatown – it's delightful. And I bought a small model of a cable-car there, for you to give to your grandson.'

'Oh, you shouldn't have Eddy, but it's very kind of you. Talk about excitement, you aren't the only one. We've been in a right two and eight here. No end of comings and goings in the street. You know little Abe Resznik, with the thick glasses, the old man who limps? Well, he's vanished! It's a regular mystery.'

'Old Abe? When was this?'

'Only last night. A right puzzle. Apparently he'd arranged to see another old codger, Bill Cooper – you know Cooper, the fat geezer who led all those strikes. Well, anyway, they'd fixed up to meet at The Three Suns last night. Abie didn't turn up so Bill Cooper went round to his place. No answer, then a neighbour she said how Abie had definitely gone off to the pub. So Cooper went back to The Three Suns, and then to all the other pubs. This morning he reports it to the rozzers. They go round to Abie's place. Bed not slept in and all his clothes are still there. Then someone finds his stick. In the High Street, just facing the Berisford Spice Mill where I used to work. They make more of a search and find his specs too, down by the water's edge. You know those old houses, Wapping Pierhead, what they're converting into posh flats. Well, Abie's specs were found on that little promenade, just where they've hung up a life-belt.'

Buchanan tried to sort out the possibilities raised by this news. The macabre resemblance to David Resznik's murder was so strong that it seemed the only answer, but what could be the link between the two murders? Then he recalled Jerry Harland at the party saying that David Resznik had written some record of what had been going on, 'names, places, dates, everything . . . fizzing away right now like a bomb with a time-fuse.' It was possible that David had put this into a letter he had written to Abe, but would a group of young revolutionaries in California have the organization necessary to arrange a murder in London? It was as baffling as the fact that professional killers had been called in to dispose of David.

Kate Johnson had paused to see if he was going to make a comment on the mystery of Abe Resznik's disappearance. As he was silent, she continued: 'Someone said something about suicide, him being so old, nearly eighty, and his eyesight very bad too, but I don't go much on that. Nor do his closest neighbours. Mrs Ferber, f'rinstance. 'Course, mind, she's rather against Abie cos he didn't bring young Davie up like a proper Jew, no *barmitzvah* or anything like that – they eat bacon like you and me. I remember her saying to me about Abie once "I'd like to buy him at my price and sell him at his own." She meant, you see, he'd got too high an opinion of himself, being very proud and so on. I'd have to agree a bit with that. I mean he is proud and he's tough, even though he's a little lame chap. That type don't never give in. What do you think, Eddy?'

'I've only spoken to him a couple of times. But I'd agree too, Kate. He seemed very independent and self-contained. Yes, and tough too. There may be some other explanation.'

'You mean that he'd gone off somewhere. No! Couldn't have without his specs! He's practically blind without 'em. The river police have been making a thorough search. But you know what it's like here. We get the poor souls who jump off Waterloo Bridge. Fall in at Wapping and you're liable to be found at Greenwich...'

Kate Johnson stopped talking and studied Buchanan as if she were making a diagnosis. 'You're feeling tired my son. You don't look your old self at all. I suppose you did go to see a doctor over there? Well, then, what about some tea and a little something to eat? I was just getting mine. I'll bring you some up.'

'Thanks, Kate. I did miss a meal somewhere on the trip. The flight was delayed from Los Angeles because of bad weather, and then it was so bumpy that several people were sick. So I'd like some tea.'

By the time he had put his clothes away and repaired the poor shave he had managed on the plane, there was a knock at his door. Kate carried in a tray. 'There! Just what I was having myself, and there was enough for two, so it was easy.'

On the tray there was a small pot of tea kept warm by a knitted woollen cosy, some thick slices of a fresh white loaf with yellow salt butter dabbed on in chunks, a small portion of smoked haddock on the bone, and a boiled egg wrapped in a napkin to eat with the fish. The haddock was firm with large flakes, and full of

134

flavour. On the rare occasions when Mrs Johnson cooked him a meal it was always something simple, with reasonably cheap ingredients, yet tasty and satisfying, having a kind of earthy quality; like steak and kidney pudding, plaice and chips cooked in beef dripping, or stewed eels with mashed potatoes and parsley sauce. Living so near to the Billingsgate and Smithfield Markets, it was easy to get prime fish and meat.

Buchanan ate the meal slowly, enjoying it just as much as the very expensive dinner Jack Collier had paid for on his last evening in San Francisco. When he took the tray down Mrs Johnson had gone out, and he returned to his own room and leafed through a copy of the *New Yorker* which he had bought in Los Angeles, but was unable to concentrate on it.

From his window at the front of the house he could see that mist was running up Tench Street like a river, bouncing off the very high blank wall which bounded one side of it from St John's Churchyard. Kate Johnson was standing talking to two other women half-way up Reardon Street, close to Abe Resznik's flat. He decided that later on in the evening he would call at The Three Suns where he would be sure to hear of any developments concerning Abe Resznik's disappearance. His mind was wandering uselessly, continually flitting from one subject to another. The type of the *New Yorker* seemed blurred. He switched on the wireless and heard Nat King Cole singing 'Because of the Rain' – the lyric seemed to have a special meaning for him, as the first time that he had made love with Laura it had been raining steadily and afterwards they had watched it beating on the window against a background of a gradually darkening sky. He lay down on the bed, held the magazine up as though to glance at it once more, then dropped it and fell asleep.

18

The screech of protesting tyres as a car was taken round a tight corner at too much speed woke Buchanan abruptly; it intruded into oblivion like a sharp memory from his past; it was as unusual a sound in Tench Street as the swishy yowl of a Ferrari Lusso or the burble of a big old Bentley. It was quite pointless to drive at speed in the maze of narrow Thames-side streets. He went to the window and saw that a white MGB had braked at the corner of Reardon Street. He watched it move off with a burst of acceleration, then brake sharply again in Watt's Street. Another car, a small dark Fiat, came along in the same direction from the High Street, pausing at the crossroads as if the driver was undecided which way to go from there, then turned after a few moments into Reardon Street and disappeared round the bend.

Buchanan recognized the driver of the MGB immediately she stepped from the car. It was Cherry Kinsella, dressed in a shiny black mac with a black roll-necked pullover and white trousers. She walked slowly towards the corner of Reardon Street with her head down, taking deliberate steps as if she were counting them. Buchanan raced down the stairs and threw open the front door. Cherry was standing still, plunged in thought, as the mist swirled around her. She looked like a fashion model transported to Wapping by a photographer who wanted to use the fortress-like walls of the Western Dock as a recherché background.

When Buchanan called out her name Cherry looked round with an expression of shock. She automatically shook her head and made a rigid aristocratic gesture of dismissal. Her usually pale face was flushed.

'Cherry! I want to talk to you. I knew you had come back to London and intended to search you out some time . . . '

'Well, don't bother.' She gave him a cold, critical look. 'You may well want to talk to me. Question is, do I want to talk to you? And the answer is no.' She turned away and began to walk down Reardon Street.

Buchanan ran after her and took hold of her arm lightly – it was the first time that he had initiated any physical contact and this was a bad moment for it. He could feel in her arm a repellent tension, but he was determined to make one point. He said: 'Have you heard about Abe?'

'Yes, this morning. You police spies don't seem to be a very efficient bunch, letting an old man be drowned while you are supposed to be keeping watch on him. But I'll say this for you, personally. You are certainly a clever and unpleasant liar! Anyone who would knock on the door at Sally's house and smarm his way in, telling lots of lies, so that he could ferret around in somebody else's room . . . Words fail me! Of course it was easy with Sally. She's too nice a person to understand that there are people capable of doing things like that. Do you mind letting go of my arm?'

'I'm going to hold it just long enough to say that I understand how you feel. And I know it must have been a terrible shock for you, hearing about David. You can believe me or not as you please, but when I heard that he was dead it was an unpleasant shock for me too. We were on different sides, if you like, but the more I got to know about him – well, he earned my respect. Look, I want to talk to you and it's important. So *please*, give me a few minutes?'

'It's just more police spying activity – that's all you want. Whatever I say will be written down later and used against some of my friends. Look, do you mind pushing off!'

'You realize that David went to the British Consulate to ask for help? That is a fact. On the fourth of this month he called in there, then vanished before they could question him about what was wrong. Obviously in the circumstances some effort was going to be made to find him. And with a little luck, if he'd been found sooner, things might have turned out differently. What would have been wrong about that?'

Cherry was silent but Buchanan knew that he had made a

telling point. She stood still instead of resisting his retaining hand. She looked at him searchingly, as if she were going to arrive at a decision in some curious feminine way as to whether he had a mean mouth or something like that. She hesitated. 'No, that's not good enough. Okay, so what you say about David going to the Consulate people may be true. Actually I do believe it. The fact remains that you must have been up to this nasty spying lark, keeping track on old Abe, long before David's trouble blew up. All that stuff you fed me about how you liked living in Wapping! I thought it was slightly queer at the time. And the sick-making notion that you wanted to do something worthwhile! Christ, this is it I suppose! Holed up in a room watching an old man.'

'I haven't any intention of trying to defend my own activities — that isn't the idea at all. And I *don't* want any information from you. I just want to tell you something I think you should know.'

Cherry sighed. 'All right. Tell me.'

'Not here. I can't discuss it here in the street. Come up to my flat — for five minutes.'

Silently she turned round and started walking. While they were crossing the road she said in a weary voice 'No other news about Abe I suppose? I mean, I heard this morning that they'd found his stick and specs.'

'No, at least according to my landlady that's still the position. And a pretty grim one it is too.'

As they walked up the dingy staircase with the threadbare carpet and damp-spotted wallpaper, Cherry had a contemplative look. He knew her mood was changing again; she was like a volatile pressure system to which he was sensitive. She walked into his bed sitting-room with the wary explorative movements of an invalid, but it wasn't because she feared an attempt at seduction; this sort of living was foreign to her. She was an admirer of revolutionaries but without any experience of working-class life. Kate Johnson's cleanliness to some extent placated the spectre of poverty, but it was still there.

The shine of fascination was in Cherry's eyes as she looked round the room; Buchanan followed her gaze that travelled slowly from the scuffed woodwork to the faded lace curtains, the pleated yellow glass shade on the light and the two vases that looked as if they might have been won at a fair. He had entertained Laura on a few occasions in this room but as it contained a comfortable double bed she had not been concerned about their surroundings, indeed it had seemed as if the sordidness added something to the sexual act by which they contrived momentarily to escape reality. He motioned Cherry towards the solitary armchair and brought a bottle of Glen Livet whisky and two glasses from the tiny kitchen.

Cherry took her glass and got up from the chair to walk to the window. 'This, presumably, is the famous spying nook, where you could keep track on what Abe was doing. Poor Abe – I still can't believe that he and David are dead.'

'It's always like that when people die. You feel they must be somewhere . . . What I wanted to say to you was about Abe. If he was killed then I think I may know why. In San Francisco I heard that David had written down all the details of this plot which apparently went wrong. I think he may have put them in a letter to Abe, and someone felt that Abe must be murdered just to keep him quiet. Don't you feel that something should be done to stop . . . '

Cherry's nose was pressed to the window as she peered towards the small block of flats where Abe had lived. She said reflectively: 'All the King's horses and all the King's men couldn't put Humpty together again . . .'

Buchanan made a rare gesture of annoyance. 'Oh sod it! We must look at things so differently that I'm just wasting your time. Perhaps it doesn't make any impression on you – such ruthlessness. Personally I think the bastards who did that . . . '

'There's ruthlessness on your side too.'

'Not like that there isn't. At least I haven't ever heard of any political prisoner being thrown into the Thames. Oh well, forget it. We'll just have this drink.'

Buchanan expected Cherry to fling out of the room but she stayed where she was and again stared out of the window as if she was enamoured of the restricted view. There was a long silence, during which he finished off his drink. Suddenly, unexpectedly, she started talking in a conversational tone: 'David did write a letter, but he didn't send it to Abe. I found it in my case the night

I went back to Laguna Street. I expect you're right. The bastards who killed him must have known of its existence. And they guessed – or that weak link Fred may have told them to save his own skin – that Abe was the one likely to get it. I'm telling you this not because I've changed my opinion of you and your work but because I'd like to hit back at those men who killed David.'

'Where is the letter?'

'It doesn't exist any longer. I burnt it. And I'm not going to say a word that will implicate any of David's friends, apart from Fred, and I don't give a damn about him now. He must have run out of that place where they were holding David. That's all he cared about in the end, just getting out. It was all his fault too. You see, he told David he had contacted someone in L.A. who was violently against the Vietnam war, someone who would finance the sabotage of defence plants all over the West Coast. Anyway, this man had come up with a plan for planting bombs in these places. Some were to be set off as a warning, and then the others were to be left in place to be exploded if Tricky Dicky Nixon wouldn't take notice. Fred talked David into it, as far as I could make out. Then David became suspicious of the plot. He found out that all the bombs were being put in places built by one firm, Enterprise Constructions Cemaceco. Enterprise is one of the biggest building firms in California. After a bit he began to suspect that the plan was to cripple that firm temporarily rather than sabotage the Vietnam war effort. He kept probing into the background of it and somehow came up with the cable address of the organization behind the plan. Quicksilver – that's the New York cable address of a great construction firm based in France called Garve-Schweber et Cie.'

A picture flashed into Buchanan's mind: of the cluttered desktop in David Resznik's room and the pile of financial column cuttings with a magnifying glass on top which had focused attention on the word FRENCH.

'So David went to Los Angeles and had it out with this man, the one Fred had contacted there. Apparently it was Jaeckel; it seems he's employed by Jean Louis Garve, a French industrialist who controls the firm. Jaeckel told David to stop probing and get on with what they'd planned. They had a flaming row and David said he wasn't going on with it. It was terribly ironic. He'd been manoeuvred into the position of being a tool for the kind of people he loathed most. So Jaeckel followed him back to San Francisco and hired that Negro you fought with at Stinson Beach – his name is Dinsdale – to make David do what they said. They took David and Fred to some crummy shack at Hunters Point. This is what Fred told his girl, I mean – about the house in Hunters Point. I heard it from Jerry. They were both beaten up there and Fred agreed to do anything. But David made a fight for it to get out and Dinsdale killed him, smashed his head in . . .'

Buchanan nodded. 'I see. So Jean Louis Garve makes his plans to extend his empire and if people don't do what they're told they end up dead. You didn't really destroy that letter? For God's sake! I mean if there was a list of places they had left bombs. Forget all that balls about the need for violence! When bombs go off people are blinded and lose their faces. Just think about that for a moment!'

Cherry's eyes were a deep clouded brown. 'I did keep a list. You can have it if you'll promise there will be no follow-up about who put the bombs there.'

'I'll settle for that. Saving lives comes fairly high on my list of priorities, believe it or not.'

'David kept a careful check.' Cherry reached in her mac pocket and produced a quarto sheet of typing paper covered with addresses – it had been screwed up and flattened out again. 'What will you do with it?'

'I shall cable it to the San Francisco Police tonight so they can start searching. I'll keep my promise and cover for you.'

Cherry put down her glass. 'It's 7.30. I must go. I'm staying with my sister-in-law in Fulham. Said I'd be back by eight.' She had a funny expression, a grimace like a clown trying to smile with a mouth that was painted with lines of sadness. 'Couldn't face living on my boat alone. Since that awful evening at Stinson Beach . . . well, I suppose I've just lost my nerve.'

They walked down the stairs in silence. Buchanan was sure that he was never going to see Cherry again, and the thought made him sad, but he could not think of anything to say which would change the position.

As they stood on the corner of Tench Street and Reardon Path, Cherry said: 'I may come here again tomorrow. Just to check about Abe . . . Will you be around?'

'I'm not sure. My plans are vague at the moment.'

'Well perhaps I'll see you. 'Bye.'

Buchanan took hold of her arm. 'The escort service continues right to the door of your car.' The mist was becoming denser and fog-horns were sounding regularly far off down the river. Buchanan noticed that a dark blue Fiat was parked in Watt's Street a little way behind the white MGB. Just before they reached the Fiat his eyes caught a movement in the doorway on the other side of the street, the flash of a face as someone turned round and tried to hide from sight. Even a glimpse was enough for Buchanan to think it was Jaeckel who was attempting to conceal himself. His pale face with the heavy widow's peak of black hair had an unforgettable dramatic quality. Buchanan did not look again, but said to Cherry: 'Well, don't over-cook it on the corners! It was the sound of your tyres squealing that brought me running to the window.'

Cherry's eyebrows shot up in mock dismay. 'Not another lecture! Well, good-bye again.'

'Turn left in Wapping Lane and you come up to The Highway which will take you to East Smithfield and Tower Hill. Your quickest way home at this time of the evening is straight through the City, Holborn and so on.' While he was giving these directions Buchanan's ears were strained to detect any sound of movement behind him.

Cherry got into the car, closed the door, then wound down the window. 'Right. Thanks Ed. See you.' She put her hand out for him to clasp.

'Yes, see you.'

The white car shot off noisily and took the left hand corner into Wapping Lane too quickly as though it was going to a fire. Immediately it was out of sight Buchanan spun round and trotted back a few paces. The man was still in the doorway, pressed to it. Buchanan ran up to him, risking the fact that he might be assaulting a Peeping Tom or some eccentric figure who had a penchant for hugging doorways.

Jaeckel turned to face him, not smiling this time but with a relaxed, confident look, like a master player beginning some game. He said: 'Well fuck you.'

'And you.' Buchanan hit him with his left, a powerful round arm punch that had floored bigger men than Jaeckel, and then a right hook. But hitting Jaeckel was an unsatisfactory matter, like wrestling with a shadow. He seemed to slip away from both punches though his position allowed little room for manoeuvre. He made no attempt to punch back but brought up his right knee towards Buchanan's groin, dived forward recklessly like someone plunging off a diving-board, turning head over heels on the pavement with the ease of a professional acrobat, then jumped up and ran off down Watt's Street.

The blow to the groin had only been a glancing one; Buchanan was as much put off by Jaeckel's audacity as by the sudden sharp pain. He had been involved in several punch-ups in his life and tackled some tough customers, but none who had Jaeckel's speed and nerve. Jaeckel had passed the Fiat and Buchanan wondered where he could be heading. Certainly in this area he must have the advantage of knowing every cobbled street and alley-way while Jaeckel would have to rely on luck. Buchanan began to pound after the dark-suited figure, remaining content to keep him in sight, saving a burst of speed till an appropriate moment.

Jaeckel turned into the High Street and then left again into Garnet Street, hesitating for a moment when he came to The Three Suns, faced by the choice of a straight street that allowed no trickery and the risk of plunging for Wapping Wall with its confusing area of warehouses which might well be a cul-de-sac. Buchanan had gained some yards before Jaeckel sped off down the covered way that led to Wapping Wall. His movements were still light and easy, like a runner doing his evening training spin. Buchanan had always been on the side of anyone against whom the dice were loaded; in films about foxes and stags being hunted he longed for them to escape their pursuers. Now he could not help feeling a grudging admiration for Jaeckel who kept his head in a very tricky situation. But that respect would not stop him clobbering the pale-faced evil figure if he could.

For the first time in the chase Buchanan heard Jaeckel's steps as he ran over the old suspension bridge across the inlet to Shadwell Basin. Jaeckel's steps did not falter again; it was as if he was being guided by some mental map. Buchanan wondered if Jaeckel could have memorized the area in case of just such an emergency. The floodlights were on over the asphalt football pitch by the King Edward VII Memorial Park and they lit up the black-suited figure as he sped past. Buchanan increased his speed. The path round the park was narrow and twisting; the park gates would be locked in the evening. He sprinted along the paved path but it seemed as if Jaeckel had somehow divined this move and ran faster too; the distance between them remained the same. Over to the right loomed the large brick superstructure that masked the pedestrian entrance to the Rotherhithe Tunnel beneath the Thames. They were right at the water's edge and the mist was heavy. At the end of the path Jaeckel disappeared and it was Buchanan's turn to stop, momentarily at a loss, turning this way and that, trying to pick up some sound. His heart was pounding and he was gasping for breath. He had thought he was fit till he competed with Jaeckel. Pointlessly he swore, mystified by the vanishing trick, then took a gamble and ran at a slower speed, with his ears cocked, towards the entrance of the tunnel. When he was within ten yards of it he heard the noise of feet clattering on the circular iron stairway which led down past the large extractor fans. His foot slipped as he began to race down the stairs, but he recovered himself without falling and ran down more slowly. The iron stairs were wet and treacherous.

Buchanan was out of breath by the time he had reached the bottom, but on emerging into the claustrophobic atmosphere of the tunnel, heavy with exhaust fumes from the continuous traffic, instead of a distant will-o'-the-wisp figure he saw that Jaeckel too had slipped and was lying on the greasy pavement. Buchanan ran up just as Jaeckel got into a crouching position, tried to grasp his left sleeve and twist it behind him in an arm-lock, but Jaeckel was extraordinarily supple and elusive so that he felt he was only grasping the clothes and not the man inside them. It was like Mr

144

Punch hitting the baby to the repeated cry of 'That's the way to do it!'

Jaeckel called out an obscene French phrase which Buchanan only half-understood as it was spoken in some strange patois. Suddenly Jaeckel leapt forward with a gleeful exclamation. He had unfastened his jacket and Buchanan fell backwards under the momentum of his own effort. Jaeckel spun round and kicked Buchanan in the stomach; he was poised to kick again, but a heavy lorry was honking its horn and slowing down as if it might stop.

Buchanan's last glimpse of Jaeckel was another taunting grin, and then he was off through the tunnel in the Rotherhithe direction. There was a lot of honking from the traffic behind the lorry and it did not stop. The kick had been skilfully directed into Buchanan's stomach and for a moment he felt as though he was going to be sick. He retched and tasted an unpleasant bile-like flavour, along with whisky and smoked fish, but did not vomit.

When Buchanan was able to stand he found that Jaeckel had disappeared from view. He looked at Jaeckel's black jacket and felt in the pockets. In the right hand one there was a handkerchief which had been soaked in jasmine perfume and a packet of Gitanes cigarettes; in the left hand one he found a pale blue envelope addressed in green ink to 'M. Robert Jaeckel, 23 rue Saint Michel, Menton'. The envelope was postmarked 'Lyons' and the letter was a very affectionate one in French from someone called Nicole who longed to see Robert again as she had some important news for him.

The jacket's inside pockets were much more rewarding: there was a *Carte Nationale d'Identité* which had been issued by the *Préfecture des Yvelines* to Robert Jaeckel, repeating the 23 rue Saint Michel, Menton, address and complete with his photograph and left index fingerprint. This documented Jaeckel's birth at Alsace on 10 March 1944. By some dark-room magic the photograph showed Jaeckel with a particularly innocent expression. The lineless face beneath the smooth black hair looked like a young boy's, innocent of guile. There was also an Air France ticket issued to Jaeckel for travel from London to Nice the following day. Buchanan had worked in Nice and was disillusioned about the South of France; normally Menton would not have been on his list of places to visit, but once he saw the airline ticket he knew that someone somewhere had picked a holiday resort for him.

19

The appearance of the Cote d'Azur is changing rapidly. Vast building projects abound; large blocks of luxury flats and municipal housing schemes along with factories and other industrial plants threaten to swamp the narrow coastal area and give it an aspect of concrete. This can be called rabid commercialism or the inevitable consequences of economic development, according to your point of view. One thing is certain: the activities of the giant construction firm Garve-Schweber et Cie are playing an important part in changing the landscape. Their concrete-mixing lorries shuttle continually along the corniches, their tastefully designed hoardings can be seen erected around vacant plots waiting to be tackled, their attractive metal plaque. depicting the winged god Mercury, is on the high wire fences which protect work in progress.

The firm of Garve-Schweber has its base in the Avenue Boyer, Menton, but it also has offices in Paris, Rome, London and New York. It expands continually. Someone in the firm must pull information from the air, or they possess a quivering communications system, as might be implied from their emblem Mercury, because they have the knack of finding firms which are going through a bad period and taking them over at a critical point.

The frontier town of Menton lies little more than half-way between Paris and Rome, where the French Route Nationale joins the Italian Via Aurelia. It extends from Cap Martin to the customs post at the bridge of St Louis. It is bordered on the south by the Golfe de la Paix and the Baie de Garavan, and on the north by the lofty spurs of the lower Alps. During the latter part of the nineteenth century and the brief Edwardian era it had a considerable vogue as a health resort, and a large English colony was established; remnants of this can still be seen today in the

statue of Queen Victoria, the streets named after Edward VII
and George V, the Anglican Church, the names of hotels such as
The Bristol, the Royal Westminster, The Balmoral.

At 7.30 a.m. on 21 October 1971, Edmund Buchanan was
standing on the jetty named after the Empress Eugenie looking up at the old town of Menton which rises tier upon tier
behind the harbour. The centuries-old houses were washed in
cream, peach and apricot, and these muted colours were particularly attractive in the early morning sunlight. Buchanan had
spent half-an-hour walking round the concrete world of the
future exemplified in the new development along the sea front to
the west. None of this could be seen from the harbour. A fishing-
boat chugged slowly past the miniature red lighthouse at the end
of the Quai Napoleon III. The sky was a pale cloudless blue with
a thin curtain of mist which would disappear under the warmth
of the rising sun. The sea was emerald green, indigo blue and,
where the sunlight caught the waves, a sequined carpet. It looked
as if it would be a perfect autumn day.

Buchanan had arrived in Nice on a morning flight the previous
day and rented a Renault from the firm for which he had once
worked. As he stood on the jetty he was remembering that period
when he had quite often visited Menton in his capacity as a
driver for the car-hire company, usually taking tourists to see
the magnificent gardens at 'Les Colombieres'. Twenty-four hours
in the South of France, and the drive from Nice to Menton, had
re-inforced his theory that the French had dumped *Le Bon Dieu*
in favour of the New Franc. But the view from the harbour had
not changed: huddled houses rising up steeply in a patchwork
of mellow colours to what had once been the esplanade of a
feudal castle; dim vaulted streets with ogee arches and, close to
the sea, ruins of walls on which the watch-towers could still be
made out.

There were always plenty of hotel rooms vacant in Menton in
October but Buchanan had chosen the comparatively small Hotel
du Midi near the old market on the sea front. It was comfortable
and had a genuinely French atmosphere which he much preferred
to the mock international spirit of the larger places. He was wearing a new shirt, a black and white check one, like the Chequered

Flag, which had come to him with the compliments of the San Francisco Police Department to replace the one ruined at Point Lobos. He carried a new white windcheater which he had bought out of expenses approved by Jack Collier.

As Buchanan walked across the Quai Bonaparte towards the rue Saint Michel the old town of Menton was coming to life with the opening of shutters, doorsteps being swept and scrubbed, voices calling from the narrow side streets. The language of some of the older people was a difficult patois, a jargon composed of French, Italian, Provençal and Arabic. He listened uncomprehendingly to a wizened old woman, dressed from head to toe in black, as she scolded a small boy.

Buchanan took a seat outside the Bar le Lido in the Place aux Herbes. With his back to the café wall he was well placed to keep No. 23 rue Saint Michel under observation without this being noticed. He ordered coffee and rolls. His vigil at the same spot on the previous evening had been rewarded with two brief glimpses of Robert Jaeckel leaving the small apartment house and returning moments later with a bottle of wine.

The coffee was hot and delicious. The rolls were fresh from the baker and there was pale, unsalted butter and apricot jam. Buchanan was enjoying his breakfast so much that he nearly missed seeing Jaeckel who appeared at 8.15 and stood on the doorstep of 23 for a few moments. Instead of his usual all black and white outfit Jaeckel was wearing fawn trousers and an aubergine-coloured leather jacket with a cream crew-necked pullover. It looked as if he might be taking a day off. Jaeckel was about five foot nine and slim, with small feet and hands. There was something unusually graceful and athletic about his posture as he lounged negligently while looking up and down the street. He turned round to call up to someone inside the apartments and then walked off briskly to the left, the direction which would eventually take him to the harbour. Buchanan felt that he might well be forsaking his breakfast only in order to see Jaeckel depart on a boat trip to Monaco, and followed him without much hope of forcing a confrontation.

Instead of walking down to the sea front Jaeckel turned left again, going up the rue des Ecoles Pie. Buchanan remembered

149

that there was a veritable rabbit-warren of steps, archways, court-yards and alleyways before coming to the Place de la Conception and the Eglise St Michel. He would have said it was the kind of place where it was virtually impossible to follow someone without being suspected. Either you would lose track of the person you followed or find yourself emerging into a little square while he was still there getting back his breath after a particularly steep flight of steps. But Jaeckel seemed to be intent on helping the pursuit, making a considerate contribution by always keeping to an even pace and never pausing or looking round. Buchanan found it was surprisingly and suspiciously easy to keep track of the aubergine-coloured jacket.

20

At the highest point in the strange old town of Menton there still remains a gate of the castle of Jean II. Where the keep once stood there is now a cemetery of which Maupassant wrote in *Sur l'Eau*: 'It was the aristocratic cemetery of Europe'.

The cemetery is on a series of narrow terraces which can be entered at three levels, with a wider area at the summit that is still being used for burials. In an odd way it is like an archaeological site in that different nationalities predominate at the various levels. The graves on the lowest terrace are largely English and Russian. Victorian taste in sentiment and decoration made the English stones crowded with ornate lettering. The Russian stones are simpler and aesthetically more pleasing, but they have both equally fallen prey to years of neglect, and now the collapsed and collapsing stones, the broken iron railings and the yawning graves demonstrate the futility of purchasing a *Concession à Perpetuité*.

Robert Jaeckel led Edmund Buchanan into the lowest terrace of the cemetery from the Montée du Souvenir, a curving sharply rising road which winds past an infants' school and an immense old stone wall with geraniums and lavender growing from the crevices. The first terrace was like an obstacle course due to two rows of cypresses planted too close together, and smothering undergrowth. Ferns, brambles, plantains, nettles and grass seemed to be competing to obtain mastery over the polychrome marbles. Buchanan had to walk along practically bent double, and he found the atmosphere claustrophobic.

There was no chance of grappling with Jaeckel and knocking information out of his sneering face in the cemetery as Buchanan could hear Italian and French voices from the main area above. All he could do was to follow in Jaeckel's tracks, and it was in effect like a guided tour: it seemed as if it might have been planned to drive home some cynical lesson about death and dissolution. Pious hopes were disappearing beneath moss and strangling ivy, records of moral and distinguished lives were being eroded to the point of illegibility.

When they came to the top it was as if they were emerging into life from the grave as the dank atmosphere of cypresses, nettles and weeds was left behind. Buchanan noticed an Italian family, dressed in their Sunday best, grouped round a recent grave, still decorated with fading flowers. The father was saying something about his uncle in a quiet voice while the mother and two children listened intently.

If Jaeckel did know he was being followed, if he had intended the excursion to the cemetery as some kind of twisted joke, then he had the good sense to keep it brief. As soon as he had passed the main area of recent graves he left the cemetery and began to walk faster. The pattern of the chase in Wapping had been altered: running through the cobbled waterside alleys there, Jaeckel's steps had been so light that it had been difficult to track him in the mist; in the asphalt streets of Menton his leather soles beat out a loud, regular pattern impossible to mistake.

Buchanan followed Jaeckel down a path and steps leading to the Boulevard du Fossan and then to the rue Henri Greville, brooding on his adversary's character, again with a sneaking kind of admiration. It seemed impossible that Jaeckel did not know that he was being followed, and it took lots of guts to walk along as he was doing, knowing that the possibility of being tackled existed all the time while the advantage lay with the man behind. Courage and unusual self-confidence – his posture when lounging in the doorway at rue Saint Michel had shown that confidence – he looked as if he were waiting and hoping for some circumstance where his talent for survival would be really stretched.

When he emerged into the main road named Avenue Boyer Buchanan found his bearings again, for he had picked up customers in that area in his car-hire days. He expected Jaeckel to turn left, which would have taken them down towards the principal business area containing offices, shops and hotels. Instead, Jaeckel suddenly sprinted across the road and then began to walk quickly in the opposite direction as if heading for the hills overlooking the town. While Buchanan was still waiting for a chance to cross the busy road he saw that Jaeckel had turned off left by a greengrocer's shop. Jaeckel did this so quickly that Buchanan suspected that at last he might lose his quarry and he raced to the corner. The narrow street taken by Jaeckel led up one of the near-by hills; it was called Chemin due Rosaire, and a metal sign indicated that the path took one to the Monastère de l'Annonciation.

Jaeckel was just disappearing round another corner, ascending some steps by the side of an elegant villa. The cages of two canaries had been set in the sun and the little birds twittered continually. A young woman was working in the garden of the villa, bending down beneath the twisted boughs of an old fig tree. The sane life of Menton was going on just as it did every day – only Jaeckel and Buchanan were bound up in a strange contest that did not make sense, acting as if they were under the spell of some mutual madness.

Buchanan turned the corner by the villa and saw that the path above him was a narrow one leading up the hill in a series of steps and paved slopes. There were villas and gardens on the right hand side, trees and bushes on the left. He walked past what looked like a large sentry box, made of blue-painted wood, and found that it was a shrine with a glass front and wrought-iron doors guarding a religious statue. It was lettered in gilt: L'ANNONCIATION.

The sun was hot and Buchanan was beginning to sweat. He could hear Jaeckel's steps clattering above him. An emaciated, wild-looking cat sprang out from a patch of fleshy-fingered mesembryanthemum and raced down the path as if its life was at stake. Buchanan gave up any hope of keeping his pursuit secret and began to run as fast as he could, but when he paused for a moment by another shrine with the lettering LA VISITATION Jaeckel's steps seemed even more distant. Buchanan ran steadily, passing a series of ever more neglected shrines – LA NATIVITÉ – LA PRÉSENTATION – LE RECOUVREMENT – L'AGONIE – LA FLAGELLATION. After passing the seventh it looked to Buchanan as if they had left the inhabited part of the hill behind – there were now trees on both sides of the path and the undergrowth was becoming progressively thicker. Higher up he could see groves of olive trees and the grey mountains behind them.

By the time he had reached the twelfth shrine Buchanan had to stop to get his breath. He had been running uphill for ten minutes and his heart was racing. The path was now of dried mud and grass, very steep and winding. He could no longer hear footsteps. A large cross and a line of cypresses were outlined against the sky, and he could vaguely make out a gate by the cross; he presumed that this would mark the site of the monastery.

Jaeckel sprang out at him from the next shrine. Buchanan saw a wild-eyed image blurred by speed, and the flash of a knife. With his left hand he threw his balled-up jacket forward, as a gladiator would have used a net, and brought his right fist up in a crude kind of uppercut with all his strength. He knew his fist had connected with rocking impact which joltingly ran right back to his shoulder. At the same instant Jaeckel's knife seared down the top of his left arm and Buchanan staggered back groggily like a comedian doing a drunk act. He would have fallen but a barrier of bushes kept him upright. Jaeckel lay spreadeagled on the path. When Buchanan hurried forward he could see that his blow had broken Jaeckel's nose. Jaeckel appeared to be in a state of shock. Bright red blood dripped steadily from his nostrils. The force of the punch would have been doubled by the speed with which Jaeckel had hurled himself forward. Blood was also running from Buchanan's arm. The knife wound extended from his shoulder nearly to the elbow but it was not deep. He found a flick-knife with a steel haft by the bushes at the edge of the path, depressed the blade and put it in his pocket.

Jaeckel's face was a dirty grey colour; his breathing was shallow and fast. Buchanan found that revenge was not sweet – it was an unsatisfactory business which left one feeling empty. The prize of revenge was as elusive as quicksilver; it had run away from the sickly looking man lying on the grassy path, and now clung about the shadowy figure of Jean Louis Garve. Jaeckel had committed the murders but undoubtedly they had been ordered by Garve.

Buchanan lifted Jaeckel into a sitting position, propping him

154

up against the side of the shrine which he found was empty and without any lettering. There was blood on Jaeckel's lips too. Buchanan said: 'Your boss. Garve. I want to see him.'

Jaeckel looked up, raising his head a little, but said nothing, staring blankly.

'Come on! You can hear all right. Where can I find Garve? Do you want me to shake it out of you?' It was an empty threat for he was loath to do anything more to the pathetic figure who looked as if he could not move.

Jaeckel tried to say something, but the task of formulating words was Herculean. When he did open his mouth he made a bubbling noise, pointing feebly up the hill.

'Come on now. I'm not that stupid. You want me to believe Garve lives at the monastery?'

Jaeckel slowly shook his head and licked his lips. Buchanan took out his handkerchief and wiped some blood from Jaeckel's mouth.

Jaeckel pointed up the hill again. 'To the left. After the road then to the left. You'll find him.'

'This had better be right because I shall be back soon. Do you understand? Then, with Garve or without, you and I are going down to the town and call in at the *Agents de Ville*. Or the C.R.S. It would be the C.R.S. wouldn't it? – I mean for an assault with a deadly weapon.'

Jaeckel opened his black eyes wide, making them look bold and mocking once more, but said nothing. Buchanan slung his windcheater over his shoulder so that it hid the knife wound. 'There will be lots to talk about. I'm sure I can find other topics that may interest them.' There was a feline quality about Jaeckel's posture; he looked like a badly wounded cat momentarily at the mercy of his captor but gathering strength to escape.

There was one more shrine, titled LA PENTECÔTE, with a painting of which only gilt stars like fleur-de-lys remained on an azure sky. A road crossed the path just as Jaeckel had described. When he reached the road he could see that the path continued steeply up to where a cross and a gate showed the site of the monastery, perched on the side of the hill. He turned left on the narrow, dusty road.

Buchanan's arm throbbed steadily as he walked along, and blood ran down over his hand. The road was approaching the wooded summit of the hill and looked as if it must wind down on the other side. He was beginning to wonder if Jaeckel had tricked him when he saw a painted sign marked PRIVÉ stuck in the scanty grass under the trees on his right. Further along the road he made out a track that ran directly up to the top of the hill. Trees grew quite densely there but he caught a glimpse of a white wall. He stopped walking and took in deep breaths of the pure air, looking at the mountains which surrounded him, and then down in the Menton direction where there was a view of the Gulf of Peace from Cap Martin to the Italian border. All the way up the hill he had smelt a mixture of herbs and wood-smoke, but now the copse was odorous of earth and pine needles. Holm-oaks, cedars and parasol-pines grew up to the great white wall, but the actual summit was dominated by giant eucalyptus trees.

After passing another sign warning strangers that the area was private, Buchanan was close enough to see that the wall was made of boulders with an equally massive wooden gate. A marble plaque was set into the wall with the name CHATEAU MERCURIE in roman letters.

The feeling of pain in his arm and the sensation of weariness dropped away and one of stealth was imposed on him instead. He seemed to glide noiselessly without effort over the rutted track carpeted with pine needles. He remembered one of his father's jokes during his amateur conjuring act: 'Now watch closely. At no time will both my feet leave the floor,' and smiled at memories of the tricks going hopelessly wrong and his father saying, 'If it was easy everyone would be doing it.' There was no doubt that he felt a bit light-headed, as if he had taken several stiff drinks in quick succession, probably due to the loss of blood and the aftermath of tension. He had no anxiety about confronting Jean Louis Garve if he could find him. It seemed to be quite a straightforward matter. Garve must be a monster, behaving like some Emperor in ancient times who had men killed on caprice. To track evil like that to its source was a rare and intriguing opportunity.

156

Pausing in the open gateway, Buchanan could see part of the house, built of white stone in a Moorish design, which was at once deceptively simple and beautiful. The setting was perfect, framed by eucalyptus trees, mountains and the sky. The rutted track turned off to the right away from the house. Over in that direction a chauffeur in grey uniform was sedulously polishing a black Mercedes limousine. It seemed improbable that he had not heard Buchanan walking into the grounds but he did not pause or look up. From far down the hill there came the sound of a police siren.

A paved path led round the house to a terrace made of marble slabs with a white stone balustrade. A magnificent eucalyptus tree at the left framed the terrace and gave it shade. Buchanan walked past it. The view was superb – a panorama of blue sky, mountain tops and glittering sea. On the other side of the balustrade there was a sheer drop down to the uncertain perspective of mountain slopes, hills and a valley road like a thin 'S'. At the far end of the terrace there was a mounted telescope. It was a fine situation for feeding a power/paranoia complex. Viewed through that telescope people on the streets in Menton would appear absurd miniscule creatures, too trivial to matter.

'On est privé içi. Vous comprenez, Monsieur? C'est une maison privée.' The slurred warning came from a squat graceless figure who had appeared noiselessly through an archway near the telescope. The man had a blank pale face and large red lips that looked as if they had been painted on. He wore a grey flannel suit with a white shirt, black tie and scarlet leather slippers.

'Monsieur Garve? My name's Buchanan. I've just been having some trouble with your man Jaeckel.'

Garve's face did not show surprise or dismay. He leant forward slightly, appearing to brood over the sunlit scene like someone playing chess. 'Jaeckel? Some mistake. You have me confused . . . Nothing to do with me.' There was no trace of accent but the bad enunciation indicated that the words had trouble getting past an obtrusive tongue. His look implied a trifling annoyance such as one might experience in being kept waiting.

Buchanan heard a police siren again and this time it sounded quite close, possibly in the monastery area. He did not speak as he took a few steps in Garve's direction. He was fascinated by this man who could make plans up on a hilltop in Menton that led to deaths thousands of miles away just to extend his concrete empire. He felt temper rising inside himself, as though he were in the grip of a fever. He said: 'No mistake. Robert Jaeckel of 23 rue St Michel, one of your employees. He's a busy little chap. I've had trouble with him in San Francisco, London and now here, right on your doorstep.' He took off his windcheater to show his bloodstained arm. 'Jaeckel stabbed me. I want you to come with us down to the town, to see the police. There's a lot to talk about. Jaeckel will talk.'

'Jaeckel will talk?' Jean Louis Garve permitted himself a bleak smile as he parroted Buchanan's last sentence doubtfully. 'No, young man, you confront me with a problem it is true. But it has nothing to do with an excursion to the town.'

'You're coming down there. That I promise you. We can make the trip in a civilized fashion, in your car if you like. But one way or the other, even if I have to lead you down there by the ear, we're going.' Buchanan moved forward again.

'Don't come any closer!' Garve's face was still devoid of expression, but Buchanan could see beads of perspiration on his long upper lip. 'Stop where you are. I have a man with a rifle behind that tree. If you were shot, that would be an easy solution for me. There are so many ravines where we could lose you . . . So!'

Buchanan shook his head, saying 'No. Not easy,' then leapt forward to grip Garve's shoulder. As he did so he heard the sharp noise of a shot and stumbled. It was just as if someone had given him a violent push in the back. The jolting blow made him feel foolishly weak. He embraced Garve with both arms. Close to there was a sickly sweet smell about Garve, and his thin hair was like a mouse's grey fur. He and Garve clutched each other like drowning men who had no idea how to save themselves. Blood was pouring down between them, equally soaking his shirt and Garve's suit.

Garve coughed and moved gently, wanting to resist the embrace but lacking any strength. His skin was now a grey colour that matched his eyes. He lifted his head up higher as though to get more air, looking at Buchanan with panic-stricken eyes that suddenly dulled. 'Careful! My heart!'

The graceful branches of the eucalyptus tree began to whirl round. Buchanan's grasp on Garve's shoulders became lighter; strength was slipping away from his fingers and leaking from his legs like the blood that flowed down them. The evil he had pursued had eluded him once more, leaving him in the arms of a sick old man. Suddenly the earth began to spin beneath his feet, and he felt as if he was on a merry-go-round which was whirling ever faster into darkness.

After what seemed only a few seconds of oblivion Buchanan opened his eyes to find that the scene about him had changed. He was still on the terrace but lying down in the shade of the tree with his head on a pillow and covered by a thick white blanket. Garve had vanished and his place had been taken by Jack Collier who crouched on his heels looking down at him with a sad expression, saying: 'You were foolish! Very foolish laddie. I told you to drop it. But by God you really follow a thing through. Now just hold on ... We've sent for an ambulance and it will be here in a few minutes. We've collected Jaeckel. I was hot on your heels all the time. And Garve will pay too. Yes, he'll pay all right. Hold on boy ...'

Collier's face was distant and distorted. Buchanan watched a small brown bird alight on the springy tip of a eucalyptus branch, then drop over the terrace balustrade into the unending blue of the sky. It was a beautiful world and man's evil, like hope and love, seemed an evanescent thing. Collier was still talking; at least he continued to open his mouth and urge some request but the only sound Buchanan could hear was that of the ocean pounding on the shore. Suddenly a voice did break through; it was very close but was too feeble and pathetic to be his own. Jack Collier, the tree and the sky all faded from view and he took his seat again on the darkening merry-go-round.